I0663785

The Keys
A YOU are the Hero book

BALOGUN OJETADE

ISBN: 0991407318
ISBN-13: 978-0-9914073-1-6

DEDICATION

To my father, Adam A. Swan and to my
mother, Almeater Swan, who always
encouraged me to follow my heart and to do
what makes me happy

ACKNOWLEDGMENTS

I would like to thank my wife, Iyalogun, for her ceaseless support and my children – all eight of them – and grandchildren – both of them – for their enthusiasm and inspiration.

HOW TO READ THIS BOOK

Warning! Warning! Warning!

Do *not* read this book straight through, from beginning to end!

Within the pages of this book is an amazing, globe-hopping adventure in which you are the hero. *You* are the one who will save the world...or destroy it.

As you read the story, you will be asked to make choices. Those choices will lead to success or disaster; to life or death.

You are responsible for what happens because *you* choose. After you make each choice, follow the instructions to see what happens to you next, but think carefully before you choose...it might be the last choice you make.

BACKGROUND

We all know of the great pyramids of Saqqara and Giza in Egypt – 138 towering, ancient monuments of stone built in tribute to the Pharaohs; and many of us even know that other cultures besides the Egyptians built pyramids – the Igbo of Nigeria; the Nuba of the Sudan; the Aztecs of South America; the Han of China; the Creek Nation in the state of Georgia, in the United States and many more – and, in fact, pyramids, or the remnants of them, still stand all over the world.

But what most people *don't* know is that the pyramids are actually portals; doors that allow instantaneous travel between each other. Using the pyramids, a boy or girl in Nigeria could visit their friend in China, 6,153 miles away, in the blink of an eye.

Each type of pyramid required a different type of 'fuel' that they required to keep running. Some pyramids required salt water; some gold; some human blood and other strange materials. Vast empires formed around pyramids that shared the same fuel requirements.

For thousands of years, there was peace between nations, who freely exchanged knowledge, culture, goods and services. All of the pyramid cultures worldwide advanced because of this exchange.

Then, in 1414 B.C., the powerful Balkan Empire – which was comprised of Greece, Turkey, Albania, Bosnia and Herzegovina, Macedonia, Montenegro and Serbia – attacked the Ajuran Sultanate, an empire that encompassed the entire 'Horn of Africa' – Sudan, Somalia, Ethiopia, Djibouti, Eritrea, Kenya and Uganda.

The attack by the Balkan Empire was an attempt to take control of the Ajuran Sultanate's pyramids, for the Balkan pyramids, powered once a year by the blood of twin boys, had not been fed in three years because no twin boys had been born in the entire Balkan Empire in all that time and they only had two journeys left. The Ajuran pyramids, however, only required an annual sacrifice of a ton of salt water. The Balkan Empire, fearing they would fall far behind the rest of the world in technology and culture and eventually be usurped by a more advanced culture, declared war on the Ajuran Sultanate.

Not expecting an attack to come during such peaceful times, the Ajuran Sultanate was caught unaware and unprepared. Within three months, the Ajuran Sultanate had suffered massive casualties and faced defeat. Not wanting to surrender totally, or to lose any more Ajuran lives, the leaders of the Sultanate offered to become allies with the Balkan Empire and to help them to wrest control of the far-reaching lands of the wealthy and powerful Oyo Empire in West Africa.

The Oyo Empire – the largest and most populated of all the empires – included the nations of what are now known as Nigeria; Liberia; Sierra Leone; Togo; Benin; Cote d'Ivoire; Ghana; Guinea; and Guinea-Bissau.

The pyramids of the Oyo Empire required an annual sacrifice of half a million cowry shells and a half ton of gold, materials found in abundance in the great

West African empire.

The Balkan Empire agreed to the Ajuran Sultanate's proposal and an army of Balkan and Ajuran soldiers prepared to journey through the Ajuran pyramids and launch a massive attack on the empire of Oyo.

At the same time, the Iberian Empire, which included Portugal; Spain; and France, attacked the peaceful Aztec Empire. Led by Infante ("Prince") Henry the Navigator, a dark-hearted sorcerer obsessed with finding the legendary Kingdom of Prester John, the Iberian Empire came down upon the Aztec Empire – comprised of Mexico; Belize; and Guatemala – with an incredible brutality.

Thousands of Aztec men, women and children fell under the swift attack of the Iberian Empire and the waterways that crisscrossed throughout the Aztec Empire, connecting their pyramids ran red with Aztec blood.

Henry the Navigator and his army marched toward the grand pyramid in Nueva Guatemala de la Asuncion ("Guatemala City"), which Henry believed was the portal to the hidden city of Prester John, Christian patriarch and king said to rule over a Christian nation in which its residents were granted immortality. Henry the Navigator intended to take control of the grand pyramid and feed it double its required annual sacrifice of the blood of 2500 warriors. Henry believed his sacrifice of 5000 warriors would provide the pyramid enough power to open the secret portal to Prester John's kingdom for a short time; enough time for him to pass through it and live in paradise on Earth forever.

The Aztec Empire asked for help from the Oyo Empire because they had always had a good relationship with Oyo and the Aztecs believed the Oyo could provide the numbers that would allow them to defeat the Iberian Empire.

Now under attack by the Balkan-Ajuran Confederation, the Oyo Empire accepted the Aztec's offer and the mighty Oyo-Aztec Alliance was formed.

With their combined military and spiritual power, the Oyo-Aztec Alliance brought the fight to both the Balkan-Ajuran Confederacy and the Iberian Empire and after a bloody battle, now known as the *War of Empires*, which lasted only thirteen days, the Balkan-Ajuran Confederacy fell and the Iberian Empire, fled back to Southwest Europe.

The ruler of the Oyo Empire, the Alaafin ("Emperor") Oranyan Shola and the Tlacocochcalcatl ("High General") of the Aztec Empire, Zaniya Xipil, conferred with their priests and oracles and it was decided that man was no longer responsible enough to handle the power of the pyramids with honor and peace, so they traveled, with their powerful combined military, from empire to empire, ordering their leaders to deactivate their pyramids. Those who complied were left in peace. Those who resisted were beaten into submission and their pyramids were destroyed.

Oranyan Shola and Zaniya Xipil then deactivated their own pyramids until the time came when man was once again ready to manage their power.

It was said that the only way a pyramid could be once again activated after deactivation was to feed it the blood of one of the Old Gods of that land. To ensure that such gods would be accessible when it was the proper time, the Aztec and Oyo priests used their formidable powers to trap the spirits of two gods – one from among the Orisha (sentient Forces of Nature) of the Oyo Empire and one from among the Teotl of the Aztecs – in the bloodline of their families, ensuring that in every generation, one member of each bloodline is host to the gods.

A guardian, called a *Locksmith,* secretly guides and protects these hosts, who are known as *Keys.*

Each Locksmith is always the child of one descendant of the Aztec Empire and one descendant of the Oyo Empire. Locksmiths are well versed in the cultures, histories, lore, languages and rituals of the people of both empires. The parents of Locksmiths are members of a secret society called the *Gatekeepers*, who ensure the Aztec and Oyo pyramids remain deactivated until man is ready, which is prophesized to be signaled by the meeting of both Keys at a new pyramid.

Now, over 600 years later, the current Locksmith is known as Sombra, a strong-willed, honorable and courageous 42 year old woman. She is a skilled warrior and bodyguard with amazing skills and abilities and heightened intellect and physical abilities.

But who are *you*?

Are you the feisty, extreme journalist, Theresa "Terry" De Fuego? Or are you the mathematical genius and basketball prodigy, Jordan Drummond?

If you choose to be Terry De Fuego, turn to page 11.

If you choose to be Jordan Drummond, turn to page 15.

THERESA "TERRY" DE FUEGO

You are Terry De Fuego, a popular video blogger who specializes in interviewing hard to reach celebrities and up-and-coming stars in sports, film and television.

You are called 'the Extreme Journalist' because you will brave danger and even bend certain rules to get your interviews, which are popular because they are blunt and funny, just like you are.

Your *most* popular interview, which has gotten over ten million views on the internet, is your exposé of lightweight boxing champion, Lloyd Marcos and his practice of paying off fighters to take a dive. Marcos, in a rage, tried to attack you and take your video camera, forcing you to defend yourself. Your camera, which stood on a tripod, captured your lightning-fast spinning crescent kick; the heel of your right foot hammering into Lloyd's jaw.

A second later, Lloyd collapsed onto

his face, unconscious.

You shrugged your shoulders, looked into the camera and said "I guess Lloyd didn't know I have been training in Capoeira Angola – an African-Brazilian martial art form – since I was three years old. He should have done his research."

Your web series, *Journey of the Extreme Journalist*, has been a hit ever since.

You are 19 years old and, although you were born and raised in the La Villita – Little Village – area on Chicago's West Side, you spent most of your summers as a little girl in Mexico City, Mexico with your abuelo y abuela – your grandfather and grandmother. Your grandparents taught you to be proud of your Mexican heritage, especially the royal Aztec warrior blood that runs through your veins.

You stand five feet, seven inches tall and weigh 143 pounds, with an athletic build that you keep well-toned through your practice of Capoeira and Parkour – a system of running, jumping and climbing for self-protection and physical fitness.

You are attractive, with dark brown, almond-shaped eyes and straight, black hair that you wear in a short, disheveled, pixie style.

Finally, you are a skilled researcher, journalist and videographer. You are also a great public speaker and are also fairly skilled in computer operation and driving a car.

Check out yourself on the next page and then continue on to page 19.

JORDAN DRUMMOND

You are Jordan Drummond, the #1 collegiate basketball shooting guard in the United States.

Although you are only 19 years old, three professional basketball teams are already interested in recruiting you after you graduate. You, however, have your heart set on being the next Streetball All-Star. You have grown bored with college and are looking for a way out; Streetball seems like a cool way to go.

Why are you bored? Because your classes no longer provide a challenge for you?

But it's not the college's fault, most colleges and universities wouldn't provide a challenge for someone who excelled in trigonometry in the 2nd Grade, while most of your peers were struggling with simple fractions.

By the time you were twelve, your parents had enrolled you in the local junior college for Calculus classes and at sixteen, you could literally *see* mathematic patterns in everything you did, which gave you the ability to determine the best play in basketball and at what angle to shoot to ensure the ball fell into the basket every time; if only you could determine whether a girl would say yes when you asked her out on a date, or the winning lottery numbers.

You keep your ability to see mathematic patterns to yourself; you don't want folks to think you're crazy, or that you somehow have an unfair advantage in basketball. Heck, even though you could see where you *should* shoot the ball, you *still* had to handle the ball and get close enough to the basket to make the shot; and you *still* had to make the shot yourself...and at that, you were still the best. Of course, your ability to see patterns allowed you to see where you should run, when you should pass and when a foul was likely to happen.

You were born and raised in Atlanta, Georgia, but your mother, who is of Igbo and Ateke African ethnicity, would tell you stories of growing up in Nigeria, where her father is from and in Gabon, where her mother is from. You would spend hours playing your mother in the Igbo mathematic strategy game, *Okwe*, called *Mancala* in some parts of the world, or in the forest, learning to live off the land like your forest-dwelling Ateke ancestors.

From your father, you learned the game of basketball and developed a love of comic books, cartoons and anime. In fact, your father is the lead animator and artist for the popular animated superhero show, *The Scythe*. You are a pretty good artist yourself and one day, when you retire from basketball, you plan to create a comic book of your own.

You stand six feet, seven inches tall and weigh 208 pounds. You have a lean, athletic build and your fast metabolism and low body fat give you a chiseled, well-defined physique. You have brown eyes and dark brown, shoulder-length dreadlocks. Your complexion is a smooth, chestnut hue.

Check yourself out on the next page and then continue on to page 26.

A shrill voice jolts you out of a good dream in which you are interviewing your idol, boxing champion, Mia Rosales St. John:

"We are now boarding flight 221, leaving O'Hare Airport at 6:00 am and arriving in Memphis, Tennessee at 7:45 am."

The flight attendant continues to speak into her headpiece microphone as she stands at the ramp door, ready to inspect tickets a final time. "Please, line up and present your ticket to me when you reach the front of the line. Thank you, for choosing Southern Airlines and enjoy your flight!"

After a brief wait in line, you board the plane and find your seat, which, of course, is a window seat – you enjoy looking at the beautiful terrain far below, imagining that you are a great eagle, soaring across the sky.

After a while, you reach into the pocket of your wind jacket and retrieve the book your mother recently gave you for your birthday – *Fist of Africa* – an action-packed adventure novella. It's a good book and you lose yourself in its gripping story. You are so into it, in fact, you don't notice when the plane begins its descent toward the Memphis International Airport.

The plane lands and comes to a smooth stop. You close *Fist of Africa* and slip the book back into the pocket of your jacket.

You grab your camera bag from the overhead compartment and exit the plane. You walk out of the airport and head toward the taxi stand.

The temperature is uncharacteristically chilly for a spring day in Memphis and you are glad you decided to wear your wind jacket.

"Need a ride, miss?"

You turn toward the voice. Leaning against a blue and white sedan is a short, chubby man with deeply tanned skin that peeks out from beneath a ridiculously thick, black beard and a huge, curly black afro that cascades down his forehead and over his eyebrows.

My name is Wali Danforth," the man says. His accent is Scottish. You recognize it because Mr. Forbes, your high school gymnastics coach, was from Edinburgh, the capital of Scotland. "And you are?"

"I'm Terry," you reply. "And yeah, I need a ride."

"Where to?" Wali asks, opening the rear passenger door.

"The Pyramid Arena," you answer as you approach Wali's car.

"Then, hop in, Miss Terry and we'll have you there in a jiffy!"

As you reach the Auction Avenue Bridge, you gasp as you see a giant, black pyramid looming in the distance.

"Ah yes, she is magnificent, isn't she?" Wali says, nodding toward the Pyramid Arena. "She stands 321 feet tall and 591 feet wide at the base, making her the sixth largest pyramid in the world."

Wali pulls up in the parking lot across the street from the arena. "There are two entrances, Terry – the front entrance usually has two security guards posted inside. They can direct you to where you need to go after you show them your press pass. The other entrance is the box office on the East Side of the building. The ticket taker can also direct you after you purchase a ticket.

You pay Wali and thank him and then you walk across the street to the Pyramid Arena.

You are close to getting that interview from the next basketball superstar, Jordan Drummond, but first you have to get inside of the arena. You don't have a press pass yet and buying a ticket to the Streetball All-Stars competition will put you in the stands, far away from the players competing for the coveted spot on the All-Stars team.

If you flirt with the security guards at the front entrance and try to convince them to let you in the press booth without a press pass, go to page 31.

If you buy a ticket to the All-Stars competition and then sneak out of the stands and to the players' locker room, go to page 34.

If you try to find another way into the Pyramid Arena, go to page 37.

You dribble the ball toward the basket. A web of criss-crossing, fluorescent red threads – visible only to *your* eyes – covers the floor of the basketball court.

One zig-zagging line glows brighter than the rest. *That* is your best option. You follow the angle of the thread toward the basket, moving with feline grace and then shoot.

The ball sinks into the net.

You look around you. As usual, no one is there yet. You always arrive before the other players, coaches, announcers and referees and you always leave after them. Your routine has been the same since you were thirteen – you come in early, shoot one-hundred times, sink one-hundred balls in the basket, shower and then greet the other players when they arrive. After each game, you wait until the last fan has left the stands and all the players have hit the showers and then you shoot another hundred baskets. You believe this routine has – and your uncanny ability to see the best approach to the basket – is why you are the best college-level shooting guard in the world and why you are sure that, one day, you will be the greatest professional basketball player in history.

You shoot another ball, this time from the free-throw line. The ball falls through the net with a crisp "pop."

"Ninety-nine," you whisper.

You dribble the ball, switching skillfully between your left and right hands. A sound, like rapid gunfire, splits the silence in the arena each time the ball strikes the highly polished maple floor. You take two steps past the three-point line and then you explode upward, leaping high into the air. You soar toward the basket with the ball held high above your head with your right hand.

You reach the basket and slam the ball through its hoop.

"One hundred!" You shout triumphantly as you land in a low, crouched position.

Clap. Clap. Clap. "Well done!"

You spin on your heels to face the source of the voice and the applause.

Standing in the seats is a middle-aged man of average height, with a lean build. His long, black fingernails are in stark contrast to his pale skin. He sports a mustache and goatee that is as gray as the immaculately combed hair on his head.

"Who are you?" You ask. "And how did you get past security?"

The man walks down the aisle in the stands toward you. He pulls a thick stack of money from the inside pocket of his black, sharkskin suit coat and taps a slow rhythm upon his palm with it. "I have my ways."

His accent is different, like one of those European villains from a blockbuster summer action movie.

"Who *are* you?" You ask again.

The man steps onto the court and saunters toward you, smiling.

You notice a strange aroma coming from him. The man doesn't stink, he just smells...strange; a smell hard to place on a human being – spicy, like a mix of evergreen, juniper and black pepper.

"My name is Henry," the man says. "And you are the great Jordan Drummond. I would wager, however, that you have no idea *how* great."

"What do you want?" You ask, taking a step back.

"To show you your greatness," Henry replies. "To teach you who – and what – you really are."

"I already know who I am," you reply. "I'm…"

"You have no idea, boy," Henry hisses. "You think that seeing patterns so that you can better toss a ball through a hoop is the limit of your abilities. You are blind to your true power. Come with me and I will open your eyes and help you see clearly."

If you take Henry up on his offer, go to page 47.

If you refuse Henry's offer and walk away, go to page 51.

You unzip your wind jacket half-way, revealing your 'Extreme Journalist' t-shirt and your well-toned, athletic body and then you saunter through one of the glass doors.

Two security guards approach you. You notice that they do not carry guns, but they are armed with extendable, steel batons, which they wear, in holsters on their belts. Two-way radios are hooked to their belts opposite their batons.

"Can we help you ma'am?" One of the officers asks. He is young, short and brawny. His pinkish, bald head reflects the ceiling's track lights.

You read his name tag before you answer. "I sure hope so, Officer Cross. I seem to have misplaced my press pass and I really need to cover the All-Star competition, or I'll probably lose my job."

"Who do you work for?" The other officer – whose name tag reads 'Marcos' – inquires.

"World Sports Magazine," you reply.

"You're lying!" Officer Cross bellows. "I wasn't sure at first, but your t-shirt gave you away – you're that girl who knocked out Lloyd Marcos...my partner's nephew."

"Oh, you're *her*?" Officer Marcos says, grabbing your arm. His sausage-like fingers dig into your forearm. Although he is much older than Officer Cross, he is extremely strong. "I don't know what you're up to ma'am, but you won't be causing any trouble around here."

Officer Marcos shoves you toward the door. "Now, go, before you get hurt!"

If you leave and head to the box office, go to page 34.

If you leave and try to find another way into the arena, go to page 37.

If you push Officer Marcos back and tell him to keep his hands off of you, go to page 46.

You walk to the box office. A young woman – just a bit older than you – sits behind a thick glass window. There isn't a line so you walk right up to her.

"Hello," you say. "I'd like one ticket to the All-Star competition, please."

"Hello," the ticket taker replies. "That'll be fifteen dollars."

You hand the woman a crisp, new twenty dollar bill through the slot in the window. She slides a ticket and a five dollar bill toward you.

"Thanks," you say, stepping away from the window.

You step over to the set of glass doors behind the box office. You tug on one of the doors; it is locked. You yank on another door; it's locked, too.

"Ma'am? Ma'am?" The ticket taker calls.

You return to the box office.

The doors don't open for another hour, ma'am," the young woman says.

You check your ticket. Sure enough, it says the doors open at 9:30am – an hour away.

"Well then, I'll take a refund, please," you reply.

"Please, check your ticket again, ma'am," the ticket taker says. "There are no refunds or exchanges."

"Thank you," you reply as you shamble away.

"Well, I guess I'll just have to sneak in," you sigh.

Go to page 37.

You walk around the outside of the Pyramid Arena, searching for another way into the building. At the back of the arena sits a small, white box truck.

Two men exit the truck carrying platters of food. Although the platters are covered, you can smell the aroma of baked chicken, sweet fruits and spaghetti. It smells good, even though the spaghetti has a bit too much basil –you have always been able to smell more clearly and accurately than most people; to hear and see more clearly and accurately, too.

Your stomach rumbles. You realize that you haven't eaten all day.

I'll eat a big meal after I get this interview, you think.

You creep to the rear of the truck, avoiding the view of the men as they carry the platters into the arena through an open door.

You peek inside the open box of the truck. There are several more platters inside and a sign that reads "Swan Catering Services."

You grab the sign and dash through the door, following the two men who carry the food, while keeping a safe distance from them so they don't spot you.

At the end of the hall stands a tall, wiry security guard.

"Good morning, ma'am," the guard says.

"Good morning," you reply.

The guard smiles and nods and you continue on your way. When you are out of his line-of-sight, you sit the sign against a wall and start searching for the locker rooms.

After a brief search, you spot a sign on the wall that says "Men's Locker Room." You creep inside the locker room and peruse your surroundings.

No one is there.

You check your cell phone – forty-five minutes before the doors open.

Jordan Drummond will enter the locker room soon. He always shoots a few baskets and then showers long before his teammates arrive and although the All-Stars aren't his teammates yet, he always sticks to that routine – a tidbit of information you received from Jordan's little sister, Zoe and it had only cost you two chocolate donuts, with sprinkles, of course.

You walk around the locker room. There are several tall lockers, with rows of wooden benches in front of them; six bathroom stalls; a row of sinks and a huge shower. There is also a door, with an 'Exit' sign above it, at the back of the locker room.

You step inside a bathroom stall, lock the door, hang your camera bag on the door's hook, remove your camera and then wait.

After a few minutes, you hear someone enter the locker room and then you hear a locker door open.

You creep out of the stall, crouch low and then sneak toward the lockers. You spot Jordan Drummond. He is pulling his sweat-soaked jersey over his chin.

You press the power button on your video camera. It quietly comes to life. You then walk briskly toward Jordan as he pulls the jersey over his eyes.

"Jordan Drummond!" You shout.

Jordan jumps and then tosses his jersey onto the bench. "What the...?"

Jordan's eyes are as wide as

saucers.

Who the heck are you?" He asks. "How did you get in here?"

"I'm Terry De Fuego," you reply, zooming your camera in to capture Jordan's shocked expression. "The Extreme Journalist; and Jordan Drummond, you are now in the Extreme Zone!"

Jordan seems to relax. He smiles and leans against a locker. "Terry De Fuego? Yeah, I've heard of you. I didn't know you were this pretty, though."

"You looked awful shocked," you say, pretending not to notice his flirtation – you hope that he doesn't notice your reddening cheeks. "Did I scare the great Jordan Drummond?"

"Well, it's not every day a woman shows up in a man's locker room and shoves a camera in your face," Jordan answers. "But honestly, at first, I thought you were a minion of this creepy guy who approached me on the court a few minutes ago."

Creepy guy?" You inquire. "Tell me..."

You pause as an elderly man enters

the locker room, pushing a cart filled with towels. The old man is tall, but walks stooped. His chubby face, toffee complexion, wavy, white hair and thick, white beard puts the image of a Black Santa Claus in your mind. You hope 'Black Santa' doesn't rat you out to security.

Don't mind ol' Sam," the old man says. "I'm just gon' stock this room with towels and the shower with soap and I'll be on my way."

"Thanks, Sam," you reply with a smile.

Sam nods and goes about his business.

"So," you continue, returning your attention to Jordan. "You were saying some creepy guy approached you?"

"Yeah," Jordan replies. "Some scary dude named 'Henry'."

"Henry?" You echo Jordan. "Henry, who?"

"Henry, the Navigator."

You snap your head toward the honeyed voice.

Standing before you is a lean, ivory-toned man with gray hair and a gray mustache and goatee. His hair and his sharkskin suit are immaculate, but his fingernails, as black as his suit, are long and uneven. A strange smell – strong to you – comes from him; a spicy aroma, like a mix of evergreen, juniper and black pepper.

You beat back the wave of nausea bubbling in your guts.

"It is rude to record someone without their permission," Henry whispers.

He waves his hand and the camera turns off. You press the power button, but nothing happens.

"What do you want, man?" Jordan asks, snatching a fresh jersey out of his locker.

"I want you to come with me, Jordan," Henry answers. "I want to teach you to tap into your true power."

Henry points a finger at you. "And, I believe you are the other Key, young lady, so I need you to come along, too."

"Umm...no," you reply.

"What *she* said," Jordan chimes in. He then slips the clean jersey over his head.

A broad smile spreads across Henry's face. "I'm afraid that I must insist."

You slip your camera into a locker and assume a low fighting stance. You begin swaying back and forth in the fundamental, triangular movement of Capoeira Angola. "You and what army is going to make us?"

Four men – identical to Henry the Navigator in every way, except for their suits, which are gray, not black – leap from Henry's torso.

"This one," Henry says, smiling.

You stop swaying and take a step back.

Jordan back-pedals away from Henry and toward the shower. "That...that's impossible! Run, Terry!"

"You won't get far," Henry snickers.

You have never seen a man duplicate himself, but you've never met a man you couldn't knock out and maybe, just maybe, if you knock Henry, or one of his duplicates, unconscious, he'll back off.

If you follow Jordan's advice and run, go to page 57.

If you kick the nearest Henry duplicate in the head, go to page 68.

"Take your hands off of me, rent-a-cop!" You scream, shoving Officer Marcos into Officer Cross. "You have no right to touch me! Do it again and *you'll* be the one hurting!"

Both security officers draw their extendable, steel batons and charge toward you.

You try to fight back, but they are on you too quickly, brutally beating you all over your body with those steel batons.

I should have found another way in, is your last thought before everything goes black.

The End

"Sure, I'll go with you," you reply.

Finally, you have a chance to escape the boredom of college and to learn more about your powers, why you have them and how you got them.

You leave with Henry, who makes good on his promise. He teaches you to see probabilities and to see the most desirable outcome in every situation.

He treats you well, but every time you ask to contact your family to let them know you are okay, he tells you that he has taken care of that and you need not worry. He doesn't allow you access to telephones, newspapers, television or the internet because, according to him, these things will just distract you from your training and development.

Your powers continue to grow until, one day, you see that every path with Henry leads to your death and to the death of thousands of others. You see that the best course of action is to leave Henry and find some young woman named 'Terry'.

You sneak out of your room in the middle of the night and creep down the long hallway toward the spiral staircase at the end of it. You check your watch; you must move with precise timing in order to avoid the horde of vicious mandrills that Henry uses to patrol the expansive grounds of his estate.

You tiptoe down the stairs and across the foyer to the mahogany double doors. You unlock the door and then pull it open just a crack. The cool night air rushes in, cooling the beads of sweat on your forehead. You slip out the door.

A single, glowing red crooked line extends from the porch to the front gate in the distance.

You leap from the porch and sprint across the grounds, following the glowing line.

Snarling Mandrills leap at you, but by following the line, you are able to evade their grasp and off-balance them.

After a few tense seconds, you reach the gate and yank it; it is unlocked. You snatch the gate open and dash through it.

You bolt through the forest just beyond Henry's mansion. After a few minutes, you come upon a winding natural path. A glowing, red line runs the length of it.

You follow the line up the path,

which leads to a huge, brick Victorian house. You dash up the stairs to the front door. You ring the doorbell, hoping that the residents will allow you to use the telephone so that you can call your parents to come get you.

The door opens...

Henry stands in the doorway, smiling broadly. "Did you enjoy your little stroll, Jordan?"

You take a step backward. Your heart races and sweat falls, in rivulets, down your face. "How...? The pattern..."

"Will *always* lead you back to me, Jordan," Henry snickers. "You still have much to learn, boy. Now, come inside. It's cold; I'll fix us some hot cocoa."

You follow Henry inside. You do as you're told. You accept Henry's teaching, waiting for the day you are finally powerful enough to escape him...

Or die trying.

The End

"No thanks," you reply. "I appreciate the offer, though. Stick around and enjoy the competition."

You turn and walk briskly toward the locker room.

What a creep, you think.

You enter the locker room and unlock your locker. Inside is a fresh pair of shorts and a fresh jersey, your street clothes and shoes and your wallet.

You begin to remove your sweat-soaked jersey.

"Jordan Drummond!"

The voice shocks you. You snatch the jersey over your head and then toss it onto the bench. "What the...?"

Standing before you is a beautiful, young woman, about the same age as you. She points a video camera at you.

Who the heck are you?" You ask. "How did you get in here?"

"I'm Terry De Fuego," she replies. "The Extreme Journalist; and Jordan Drummond, you are now in the Extreme Zone!"

You recognize her name and the

name of her show.

"Terry De Fuego? Yeah, I've heard of you," you say, leaning against a locker and flashing Terry a smile. "I didn't know you were this pretty, though."

"You looked awful shocked," Terry replies. "Did I scare the great Jordan Drummond?"

She's trying to pretend like she didn't notice me flirting, you think. *But look at her turning all red.*

"Well, it's not every day a woman shows up in a man's locker room and shoves a camera in your face," you answer. "But honestly, at first, I thought you were a minion of this creepy guy who approached me on the court a few minutes ago."

Creepy guy?" Terry inquires. "Tell me..."

She pauses, mid-sentence and stares at something behind you. You look over your shoulder. An elderly man has entered the locker room. He pushes a cart filled with towels. The old man is tall, but walks stooped.

Don't mind ol' Sam," the old man says. "I'm just gon' stock this room with towels and the shower with soap and I'll be on my way."

"Thanks, Sam," Terry replies with a smile.

Sam nods and goes about his business.

"So," Terry continues, returning her attention to you. "You were saying some creepy guy approached you?"

"Yeah," you reply. "Some scary dude named 'Henry'."

"Henry?" Terry says, echoing you. "Henry, who?"

"Henry, the Navigator."

You turn toward Henry.

Terry starts to turn a little green and sweat runs down her cheeks. Must be Henry's strange odor getting to her.

"It is rude to record someone without their permission," Henry whispers.

He waves his hand and the camera turns off. Terry presses the power button furiously, but nothing happens. The camera is dead.

How did he do that? You wonder.

"What do you want, man?" you ask, snatching the fresh jersey out of your locker.

"I want you to come with me, Jordan," Henry answers. "I want to teach you to tap into your true power."

Henry points a finger at Terry. "And, I believe you are the other Key, young lady, so I need you to come along, too."

"Umm...no," she replies.

You admire her guts. *After I win this competition and a spot on the All-Star team, I'll take her out and celebrate.*

"What *she* said," you chime in. You then slip the clean jersey over your head.

A broad smile spreads across Henry's face. "I'm afraid that I must insist."

Terry slips her camera into a locker and drops into a low fighting stance. She starts swaying back and forth like those African martial arts dudes you saw demonstrating at the Black History Festival last year. *They called it 'Kaparilla', or 'Kapo-area', or something like that.*

"You and what army is going to make us?" Terry hisses.

Four men – identical to Henry the Navigator in every way, except for their suits, which are gray, not black – leap from Henry's torso.

"This one," Henry says, smiling.

Terry stops swaying and takes a step back.

Frightened, you back-pedal away from Henry and toward the shower. "That...that's impossible! Run, Terry!"

"You won't get far," Henry says.

If you run, go to page 79.

If you stand with Terry and fight, go to page 89.

You turn toward Jordan and follow him toward the exit door at the back of the locker room.

Henry and his duplicates give chase. They weave between the lockers and come at you from all sides, but Jordan masterfully evades their grasp, as if he knows exactly where to move to avoid them.

You reach the back door. Sam, the old janitor, blocks your path.

Oh no, 'Black Santa' is one of these crazy guys, you think. But, to your surprise – and relief – Sam opens the door for you.

"Wait for me in the parking lot just beyond the next door, at the end of the hallway!"

Jordan darts through the doorway. Before you can follow him, one of Henry's duplicates charges toward you from your left.

Sam leaps in front of you, thrusting forward with a powerful flying knee strike. The old man's right knee hammers into the Henry duplicate's sternum. A loud, cracking noise follows.

The Henry duplicate collapses to his

knees.

Agonized screams fill the locker room.

Henry and his duplicates must feel each other's pain, you contemplate.

Sam raises his right elbow above his head and then snaps it down, slamming the hard, bony tip of his elbow onto the crown of the Henry duplicate's head.

The Henry duplicate's eyes roll up into his skull and his shoulders twitch. He then collapses onto his face, convulses once, twice and then goes limp.

More screams fill the locker room.

"No," you hear Henry sob.

"Run," Sam commands. "While Henry is stunned!"

You run out of the door and then dart to your left down the hallway. Sam is hot on your heels.

At the end of the hall, Jordan holds the exit door open. "Come on, y'all," he shouts. "Hurry, before that creep and his creepy clones are on us!"

You sprint out the door into the parking lot. Jordan follows you out, letting the door slam shut behind him.

Sam runs to a beat up, lemon-yellow station wagon that looks older than your abuela's abuela – your granny's granny.

You follow Sam to the car and hop in the back seat. Jordan slides in beside you.

The station wagon roars to life. Your head snaps back as Sam speeds out of the parking lot, the tires of the station wagon screeching as Sam hard rights turn onto the street.

"You fight well and move pretty quickly for an old man," you say.

"Elderly *gentleman*," Jordan says, nudging you with his elbow.

"I'm not an old man, *or* an elderly gentleman," Sam replies. His voice goes from a hoarse baritone to an appealing, feminine one.

"What the heck just happened to your voice?" You ask, shooting a glance at Jordan, whose chin has fallen to his chest.

Sam claws at his face. Chunks of flesh fall away, revealing the face of a beautiful woman underneath layers of latex makeup and prosthetics. The woman who was Sam snatches the wig from her head and tosses it into the front passenger seat. Her real hair is black, curly and cut very short.

"My name is Sombra, not Sam," the woman says. "And I'm going to keep both of you safe."

"Safe from what?" You ask. "From Henry?"

"And the monstrosities that he has brought into this world to serve him," Sombra answers.

"What does Henry want with us?" Jordan inquires.

"You are the Keys," Sombra replies. "Hosts of gods who serve the mighty and eternal Aztec and Oyo Empires."

"O...kay," you say, rolling your eyes. "The Crazy Train just left the station."

"You just witnessed a man's duplicates leap out of his chest," Sombra replies. "Was that a hallucination? Did you both imagine that? A man can do *that*, but cannot be a god in flesh? How little you think of yourself."

"Look lady," you say, wagging a

finger at her. "All this killing, monsters and mumbo-jumbo is new to me, so forgive me if I find it all a bit nuts!"

"The whole world is nuts," Sombra sighs. "It *has* been for a long time. It's broken, but we are going to mend it."

"Where are you taking us?" Jordan asks.

"To a place where we can hide, rest and I can help you understand what is going on and who you are," Sombra replies.

"Hide?" You snicker. "We're driving around Memphis in a big, yellow station wagon."

"Who would suspect us to choose such a conspicuous vehicle?" Sombra replies. "Henry will be searching for a dark vehicle. The police probably will be too."

"The police?" Jordan inquires, swallowing hard. "Why would the police be involved?"

"Because she killed one of the Henrys," you reply.

"K-killed?" Jordan gasps. "You murdered someone?"

"Not murdered," Sombra replies. "*Killed*, as Terry said. Murder is the taking of an innocent life. The Henry duplicate was far from innocent. If I had not killed him, Terry would have been taken. Nevertheless, the police will investigate and they will be looking for you."

"Us? Why?" You ask. "*You* killed him!"

"Because there were cameras in the hallway behind the locker room," Sombra answers.

"Then they'll be looking for you, too," you say.

"No, they won't," Sombra replies. "There are medicines in me that make me...elusive to electronic detection."

"Great," you sigh. "We're not only being chased by some magical creep, we're also persons of interest in a murder case."

"My parents are going to *freak*," Jordan says. "We need to stop somewhere so I can call them."

"We're here," Sombra says, pulling into the parking lot of a squalid motel. A yellow sign that reads "DANGER! This structure is declared unsafe for human occupancy or use," is glued to the office door.

Sombra drives the station wagon around to the back of the motel, away from the main street. She parks next to the dumpster. The wagon sputters, coughs and then goes silent.

"Okay, follow me," Sombra says, opening her door. "Don't say a word until we are inside."

Sombra slides out of the car and walks briskly toward the motel. You and Jordan follow her.

Sombra approaches a door marked '112'. She unlocks the door and enters the motel room. You follow her inside. Jordan enters the room and locks the door behind him.

The capacious room is surprisingly clean. Strange, brilliantly-colored symbols cover the walls and ceiling. Two full-sized beds, an oxblood leather chair, a sofa, a chest of drawers and a wide-screen, plasma television decorate the room.

"Make yourselves comfortable," Sombra says, heading toward the bathroom. "I have to remove the rest of this makeup and change clothes."

Sombra closes the door to the

restroom. You hear the click of the lock.

"I have to call home," Jordan whispers as he creeps around the room. "I don't see a phone! Where is the phone?"

"Calm down!" You reply, careful to keep your voice at a low volume. "We need to wait until Sombra comes back out and then demand some straight answers."

"Straight answers?" Jordan hisses. "We don't know her. How can we trust her?"

"We don't know each *other*," you say. "But we have to rely on each other until we can sort this all out."

"I guess you're right," Jordan replies as he rummages through the chest of the drawers. "We're in..."

Jordan's words seem to lodge in his throat. His eyes grow wide and his jaw falls slack. "O...M...G!"

"What is it?" You inquire. "Jordan, what's wrong?"

"We have to get out of here," Jordan gasps. "Look!"

He pulls a small, black leather bag – like the old school doctor's bags – from a drawer and tosses it on the bed.

You peek inside the bag, which contains a bottle of ether, two small bottles of morphine, several syringes and needles, a roll of duct tape and a bundle of plastic, disposable restraints. "What the...?"

"Exactly," Jordan chimes in. "Is Sombra saving us...or en*slaving* us?"

You cannot deny that all of the items in the bag are for knocking out or restraining a person.

"We should get out of here, now!" Jordan says.

"And go where?" You ask. "The police think we're murderers."

"We can go to the police ourselves," Jordan answers. "Take that bag; convince them we were taken hostage by the *real* murderer."

"Are you serious?" You say, shaking your head. "Where did *you* grow up? You're African-American and I'm Afro-Mexican – in the eyes of the police, we're guilty, until proven innocent."

"Well, we have to do *something*," Jordan replies. "Either we make Sombra tell us everything – including why she has a bag full of knockout drugs and plastic handcuffs – or, we take the bag to the police as evidence and allow the courts to prove our innocence."

If you restrain Sombra and make her talk, go to page 100.

If you turn yourself – and Sombra's bag – in to the police, go to page 133.

Your Capoeira instructor always said "Avoidance is the highest level of self-defense...but if you absolutely can't avoid 'em, then hit 'em hard!"

With your mestre's words in mind, you twist your hips hard to the right as you thrust your chest toward the floor. You pivot on your hands, whipping your left leg in a wide arc. Your left heel slams into the side of a Henry duplicate's neck.

The duplicate tumbles over the bench. His back hits the floor with a dull thud.

Henry and the other duplicates clutch at their necks as they scream in agony.

The duplicate you kicked begins to struggle to his knees. His eyes are glazed over and slightly crossed.

"Run!"

You whirl toward the voice. The old janitor, Sam, holds the rear exit door open.

"They won't be dazed long," Sam says. "Run, while you still can!"

Jordan sprints out the door.

"Wait for me in the parking lot, just beyond the door at the end of the hallway!" Sam orders.

You run to the door, but before you can cross the threshold, one of Henry's duplicates charges at you from your left.

Sam leaps in front of you, thrusting forward with a powerful flying knee strike. The old man's right knee hammers into the Henry duplicate's sternum. A loud, cracking noise follows.

The Henry duplicate collapses to his knees.

Agonized screams fill the locker room.

Henry and his duplicates must feel each other's pain, you contemplate.

Sam raises his right elbow above his head and then snaps it down, slamming the hard, bony tip of his elbow onto the crown of the Henry duplicate's head.

The Henry duplicate's eyes roll up into his skull and his shoulders twitch. He then collapses onto his face, convulses once, twice and then goes limp.

More screams fill the locker room.

"No," you hear Henry sob.

"Run," Sam commands. "While Henry is stunned!"

You run out of the door and then dart to your left down the hallway. Sam is hot on your heels.

At the end of the hall, Jordan holds the exit door open. "Come on, y'all," he shouts. "Hurry, before that creep and his creepy clones are on us!"

You sprint out the door into the parking lot. Jordan follows you out, letting the door slam shut behind him.

Sam runs to a beat up, lemon-yellow station wagon that looks older than your abuela's abuela – your granny's granny.

You follow Sam to the car and hop in the back seat. Jordan slides in beside you.

The station wagon roars to life. Your head snaps back as Sam speeds out of the parking lot, the tires of the station wagon screeching as Sam hard right turns onto the street.

"You fight well and move pretty quickly for an old man," you say.

"Elderly *gentleman*," Jordan says, nudging you with his elbow.

"I'm not an old man, *or* an elderly gentleman," Sam replies. His voice shifts from a hoarse baritone to an appealing, feminine one.

"What the heck just happened to your voice?" You ask, shooting a glance at Jordan, whose jaw has fallen to his chest.

Sam claws at his face. Chunks of flesh fall away, revealing the face of a beautiful woman underneath layers of latex makeup and prosthetics. The woman who was Sam snatches the wig from her head and tosses it into the front passenger seat. Her real hair is black, curly and cut very short.

"My name is Sombra, not Sam," the woman says. "And I'm going to keep both of you safe."

"Safe from what?" You ask. "From Henry?"

"And the monstrosities that he has brought into this world to serve him," Sombra answers.

"What does Henry want with us?" Jordan inquires.

"You are the Keys," Sombra replies. "Hosts of gods who serve the mighty and eternal Aztec and an Oyo Empires."

"O...kay," you say, rolling your eyes. "The Crazy Train just left the station."

"You just witnessed a man's duplicates leap out of his chest," Sombra replies. "Was that a hallucination? Did you both imagine that? A man can do *that*, but cannot be a god in flesh? How little you think of yourself."

"Look lady," you say, wagging a finger at her. "All this killing, monsters and mumbo-jumbo is new to me, so forgive me if I find it all a bit nuts!"

"The whole world is nuts," Sombra sighs. "It *has* been for a long time. It's broken, but we are going to mend it."

"Where are you taking us?" Jordan asks.

"To a place where we can hide, rest and I can help you understand what is going on and who you are," Sombra replies.

"Hide?" You snicker. "We're driving around Memphis in a big, yellow station wagon."

"Who would suspect us to choose such a conspicuous vehicle?" Sombra replies. "Henry will be searching for a dark vehicle. The police probably will be too."

"The police?" Jordan inquires, swallowing hard. "Why would the police be involved?"

"Because she killed one of the Henrys," you reply.

'K-killed?' Jordan gasps. "You murdered someone?"

"Not murdered," Sombra replies. "*Killed*, as Terry said. Murder is the taking of an innocent life. The Henry duplicate was far from innocent. If I had not killed him, Terry would have been taken. Nevertheless, the police will investigate and they will be looking for you."

"Us? Why?" You ask. "*You* killed him!"

"Because there were cameras in the hallway behind the locker room," Sombra answers.

"Then they'll be looking for you, too," you say.

"No, they won't," Sombra replies. "There are medicines in me that make me…elusive to electronic detection."

"Great," you sigh. "We're not only being chased by some magical creep, we're also persons of interest in a murder case."

"My parents are going to *freak*," Jordan says. "We need to stop somewhere so I can call them."

"We're here," Sombra says, pulling into the parking lot of a squalid motel. A yellow sign that reads "DANGER! This structure is declared unsafe for human occupancy or use," is glued to the office door.

Sombra drives the station wagon around to the back of the motel, away from the main street. She parks next to the dumpster. The car sputters, coughs and then goes silent.

"Okay, follow me," Sombra says, opening her door. "Don't say a word until we are inside."

Sombra slides out of the car and walks briskly toward the motel. You and Jordan follow her.

Sombra approaches a door marked '112'. She unlocks the door and enters the motel room. You follow her inside. Jordan enters the room and locks the door behind him.

The capacious room is surprisingly clean. Strange, brilliantly-colored symbols cover the walls and ceiling. Two full-sized beds, an oxblood leather chair, a sofa, a chest of drawers and a wide-screen, plasma television decorate the room.

"Make yourselves comfortable," Sombra says, heading toward the bathroom. "I have to remove the rest of this makeup and change clothes."

Sombra closes the door to the restroom. You hear the click of the lock.

"I have to call home," Jordan whispers as he creeps around the room. "I don't see a phone! Where is the phone?"

"Calm down!" You reply, careful to keep your voice at a low volume. "We need to wait until Sombra comes back out and then demand some straight answers."

"Straight answers?" Jordan hisses. "We don't know her. How can we trust her?"

"We don't know each *other*," you say. "But we have to rely on each other until we can sort this all out."

"I guess you're right," Jordan replies

as he rummages through the chest of the drawers. "We're in..."

Jordan's words seem to lodge in his throat. His eyes grow wide and his jaw falls slack. "O...M...G!"

"What is it?" You inquire. "Jordan, what's wrong?"

"We have to get out of here," Jordan gasps. "Look!"

He pulls a small, black leather bag – like the old school doctor's bags – from a drawer and tosses it on the bed.

You peek inside the bag, which contains a bottle of ether, two small bottles of morphine, several syringes and needles, a roll of duct tape and a bundle of plastic, disposable restraints. "What the...?"

"Exactly," Jordan chimes in. "Is Sombra saving us...or en*slaving* us?"

You cannot deny that all of the items in the bag are for knocking out or restraining a person.

"We should get out of here, now!" Jordan says.

"And go where?" You ask. "The

police think we're murderers."

"We can go to the police ourselves," Johnson answers. "Take that bag; convince them we were taken hostage by the *real* murderer."

"Are you serious?" You say, shaking your head. "Where did *you* grow up? You're African-American and I'm Afro-Mexican – in the eyes of the police, we're guilty, until proven innocent."

"Well, we have to do *something*," Jordan replies. "Either we make Sombra tell us everything – including why she has a bag full of knockout drugs and plastic handcuffs – or, we take the bag to the police as evidence and allow the courts to prove our innocence."

If you restrain Sombra and make her talk, go to page 100.

If turn yourself – and Sombra's bag – in to the police, go to page 133.

You tap Terry on the shoulder and spin on your heels toward the rear exit door. You leap over the bench and sprint toward the door, following the glowing, red line extending from your feet to the rear of the locker room.

Henry and his duplicates give chase. They weave between the lockers and come at you from all sides, but by following the zigzagging red line, you masterfully evade their grasp.

You reach the back door. Sam, the old janitor, blocks your path.

Don't tell me this old man is with that creep back there, you think. But, to your surprise – and relief – Sam opens the door for you.

"Wait for me in the parking lot just beyond the next door, at the end of the hallway!"

You dart through the doorway and sprint down the hall toward the door at the end of it. You push on the door, it is unlocked. You hold it open and wait for Terry and Sam.

You here crashing noises, followed by a chorus of agonized screams. The screams sound masculine. Was Terry in there beating the stew out of Henry and his minions? You weren't going back to find out.

"If they don't come soon, I'm out of here," you whisper. You've always been a team player, but you also know that you have to look out for number one first and foremost.

"Run," you hear Sam command. "While Henry is stunned!"

Terry runs out of the locker room and then sprints toward you. Sam is hot on her heels.

"Come on, y'all," you shout. "Hurry, before that creep and his creepy clones are on us!"

Terry and Sam sprint past you. You follow them, letting the door slam shut behind you.

Sam runs to a beat up, lemon-yellow station wagon. You follow Sam to the car and hop in the back seat. Jordan slides in beside you.

The station wagon roars to life. Your head snaps back as Sam speeds out of the parking lot, the tires of the station wagon screeching as Sam hits a hard right turn onto the street.

"You fight well and move pretty quickly for an old man," Terry says.

"Elderly *gentleman*," you say, nudging Terry with your elbow.

Man, she's rude, you think.

"I'm not an old man, *or* an elderly gentleman," Sam replies. His voice morphs from a hoarse baritone to an appealing, feminine one.

"What the heck just happened to your voice?" Terry asks, shooting a glance at you.

Sam claws at his face. Chunks of flesh fall away, revealing the face of a beautiful woman underneath layers of latex makeup and prosthetics. The woman who was Sam snatches the wig from her head and tosses it into the front passenger seat. Her real hair is black, curly and cut very short.

"My name is Sombra, not Sam," the woman says. "And I'm going to keep both of you safe."

"Safe from what?" Terry asks. "From Henry?"

"And the monstrosities that he has brought into this world to serve him,"

Sombra answers.

"What does Henry want with us?" You inquire.

"You are the Keys," Sombra replies. "Hosts of gods who serve the mighty and eternal Aztec and an Oyo Empires."

Uh-oh, you think. *She's nuttier than squirrel poop.*

"O...kay," Terry says, rolling her eyes. "The Crazy Train just left the station."

"You just witnessed a man's duplicates leap out of his chest," Sombra replies. "Was that a hallucination? Did you both imagine that? A man can do *that*, but cannot be a god in flesh? How little you think of yourself."

"Look lady," Terry says, wagging a finger at her. "All this killing, monsters and mumbo-jumbo is new to me, so forgive me if I find it all a bit nuts!"

"The whole world is nuts," Sombra sighs. "It *has* been for a long time. It's broken, but we are going to mend it."

"Where are you taking us?" You ask.

"To a place where we can hide, rest

and I can help you understand what is going on and who you are," Sombra replies.

"Hide?" Terry snickers. "We're driving around Memphis in a big, yellow station wagon."

"Who would suspect us to choose such a conspicuous vehicle?" Sombra replies. "Henry will be searching for a dark vehicle. The police probably will be too."

"The police?" You inquire, swallowing hard. "Why would the police be involved?"

"Because she killed one of the Henrys," Terry replies.

"K-killed?" You gasp. "You murdered someone?"

"Not murdered," Sombra replies. "*Killed*, as Terry said. Murder is the taking of an innocent life. The Henry duplicate was far from innocent. If I had not killed him, Terry would have been taken. Nevertheless, the police will investigate and they will be looking for you."

"Us? Why?" Terry asks. "*You* killed him!"

"Because there were cameras in the

hallway behind the locker room," Sombra answers.

"Then they'll be looking for you, too," Terry says.

"No, they won't," Sombra replies. "There are medicines in me that make me...elusive to electronic detection."

"Great," Terry sighs. "We're not only being chased by some magical creep, we're also persons of interest in a murder case."

"My parents are going to *freak*," you says. "We need to stop somewhere so I can call them."

"We're here," Sombra says, pulling into the parking lot of a squalid motel. A yellow sign that reads "DANGER! This structure is declared unsafe for human occupancy or use," is glued to the office door.

Sombra drives the station wagon around to the back of the motel, away from the main street. She parks next to the dumpster. The car sputters, coughs and then goes silent.

"Okay, follow me," Sombra says, opening her door. "Don't say a word until we are inside."

Sombra slides out of the car and walks briskly toward the motel. You and Jordan follow her.

Sombra approaches a door marked '112'. She unlocks the door and enters the motel room. Terry follows her inside. You enter the room and lock the door behind you.

The capacious room is surprisingly clean. Strange, brilliantly-colored symbols cover the walls and ceiling. Two full-sized beds, an oxblood leather chair, a sofa, a chest of drawers and a wide-screen, plasma television decorate the room.

"Make yourselves comfortable," Sombra says, heading toward the bathroom. "I have to remove the rest of this makeup and change clothes."

Sombra closes the door to the restroom. You hear the click of the lock.

"I have to call home," you whisper as you creep around the room. "I don't see a phone! Where is the phone?"

"Calm down!" Terry replies. "We need to wait until Sombra comes back out and then demand some straight answers."

"Straight answers?" You hiss. "We don't know her. How can we trust her?"

"We don't know each *other*," Terry says. "But we have to rely on each other until we can sort this all out."

"I guess you're right," you reply as you rummage through the chest of drawers. "We're in..."

You find a small, leather bag in one of the drawers. You open the bag and examine its contents – a bottle of ether, two small bottles of morphine, several syringes and needles, a roll of duct tape and a bundle of plastic, disposable restraints.

Your words seem to lodge in your throat, as if you have a rough-hewn stone stuck in your esophagus. "O...M...G!"

"What is it?" Terry inquires. "Jordan, what's wrong?"

"We have to get out of here," you gasp. "Look!"

You pull the bag from the drawer and toss it on the bed.

Terry peeks inside the bag. "What the...?"

"Exactly," you chime in. "Is Sombra saving us...or en*slaving* us? We should get out of here, now!"

"And go where?" Terry asks. "The police think we're murderers."

"We can go to the police ourselves," you answer. "Take that bag; convince them we were taken hostage by the *real* murderer."

"Are you serious?" Terry says, shaking her head. "Where did *you* grow up? You're African-American and I'm Afro-Mexican – in the eyes of the police, we're guilty, until proven innocent."

"Well, we have to do *something*," you reply. "Either we make Sombra tell us everything – including why she has a bag full of knockout drugs and plastic handcuffs – or, we take the bag to the police as evidence and allow the courts to prove our innocence."

If you restrain Sombra and make her talk, go to page 117.

If you turn yourself – and Sombra's bag – in to the police, go to page 137.

Lightning fast, Terry whips her left leg around in a wide arc. The heel of her left foot slams into the side of a Henry duplicate's neck.

The duplicate tumbles over the bench. His back hits the floor with a dull thud.

Henry and the other duplicates clutch at their necks as they scream in agony.

The duplicate Terry kicked begins to struggle to his knees. His eyes are glazed over and slightly crossed.

"Run!"

You peer over your shoulder, toward the voice. The old janitor, Sam, holds the rear exit door open.

You tap Terry on the shoulder and spin on your heels toward the rear exit door. You leap over the bench and sprint toward the door, following the glowing, red line extending from your feet to the rear of the locker room.

Henry and his duplicates give chase. They weave between the lockers and come at you from all sides, but by following the zigzagging red line, you masterfully evade their grasp.

You reach the back door. Sam, the old janitor, blocks your path.

Don't tell me this old man is with that creep back there, you think. But, to your surprise – and relief – Sam opens the door for you.

"Wait for me in the parking lot just beyond the next door, at the end of the hallway!"

You dart through the doorway and sprint down the hall toward the door at the end of it. You push on the door, it is unlocked. You hold it open and wait for Terry and Sam.

You here crashing noises, followed by a chorus of agonized screams. The screams sound masculine. Was Terry in there beating the stew out of Henry and his minions? You weren't going back to find out.

"If they don't come soon, I'm out of here," you whisper. You've always been a team player, but you also know that you have to look out for number one first and foremost.

"Run," you hear Sam command. "While Henry is stunned!"

Terry runs out of the locker room

and then sprints toward you. Sam is hot on her heels.

"Come on, y'all," you shout. "Hurry, before that creep and his creepy clones are on us!"

Terry and Sam sprint past you. You follow them, letting the door slam shut behind you.

Sam runs to a beat up, lemon-yellow station wagon. You follow Sam to the car and hop in the back seat. Terry slides in beside you.

The station wagon roars to life. Your head snaps back as Sam speeds out of the parking lot, the tires of the station wagon screeching as Sam hard rights turn onto the street.

"You fight well and move pretty quickly for an old man," Terry says.

"Elderly *gentleman*," you say, nudging Terry with your elbow.

Man, she's rude, you think.

"I'm not an old man, *or* an elderly gentleman," Sam replies. His voice morphs from a hoarse baritone to an appealing, feminine one.

"What the heck just happened to your voice?" Terry asks, shooting a glance at you.

Sam claws at his face. Chunks of flesh fall away, revealing the face of a beautiful woman underneath layers of latex makeup and prosthetics. The woman who was Sam snatches the wig from her head and tosses it into the front passenger seat. Her real hair is black, curly and cut very short.

"My name is Sombra, not Sam," the woman says. "And I'm going to keep both of you safe."

"Safe from what?" Terry asks. "From Henry?"

"And the monstrosities that he has brought into this world to serve him," Sombra answers.

"What does Henry want with us?" You inquire.

"You are the Keys," Sombra replies. "Hosts of gods who serve the mighty and eternal Aztec and an Oyo Empires."

Uh-oh, you think. *She's nuttier than squirrel poop.*

"O...kay," Terry says, rolling her

eyes. "The Crazy Train just left the station."

"You just witnessed a man's duplicates leap out of his chest," Sombra replies. "Was that a hallucination? Did you both imagine that? A man can do *that*, but cannot be a god in flesh? How little you think of yourself."

"Look lady," Terry says, wagging a finger at her. "All this killing, monsters and mumbo-jumbo is new to me, so forgive me if I find it all a bit nuts!"

"The whole world is nuts," Sombra sighs. "It *has* been for a long time. It's broken, but we are going to mend it."

"Where are you taking us?" You ask.

"To a place where we can hide, rest and I can help you understand what is going on and who you are," Sombra replies.

"Hide?" Terry snickers. "We're driving around Memphis in a big, yellow station wagon."

"Who would suspect us to choose such a conspicuous vehicle?" Sombra replies. "Henry will be searching for a dark vehicle. The police probably will be too."

"The police?" You inquire, swallowing hard. "Why would the police be involved?"

"Because she killed one of the Henrys," Terry replies.

"K-killed?" You gasp. "You murdered someone?"

"Not murdered," Sombra replies. "*Killed*, as Terry said. Murder is the taking of an innocent life. The Henry duplicate was far from innocent. If I had not killed him, Terry would have been taken. Nevertheless, the police will investigate and they will be looking for you."

"Us? Why?" Terry asks. "*You* killed him!"

"Because there were cameras in the hallway behind the locker room," Sombra answers.

"Then they'll be looking for you, too," Terry says.

"No, they won't," Sombra replies. "There are medicines in me that make me...elusive to electronic detection."

"Great," Terry sighs. "We're not only being chased by some magical creep, we're also persons of interest in a murder case."

"My parents are going to *freak*," you say. "We need to stop somewhere so I can call them."

"We're here," Sombra says, pulling into the parking lot of a squalid motel. A yellow sign that reads "DANGER! This structure is declared unsafe for human occupancy or use," is glued to the office door.

Sombra drives the station wagon around to the back of the motel, away from the main street. She parks next to the dumpster. The wagon sputters, coughs and then goes silent.

"Okay, follow me," Sombra says, opening her door. "Don't say a word until we are inside."

Sombra slides out of the car and walks briskly toward the motel. You and Terry follow her.

Sombra approaches a door marked '112'. She unlocks the door and enters the motel room. Terry follows her inside. You enter the room and lock the door behind you.

The capacious room is surprisingly clean. Strange, brilliantly-colored symbols cover the walls and ceiling. Two full-sized beds, an oxblood leather chair, a sofa, a chest of drawers and a wide-screen, plasma television decorate the room.

"Make yourselves comfortable," Sombra says, heading toward the bathroom. "I have to remove the rest of this makeup and change clothes."

Sombra closes the door to the restroom. You hear the click of the lock.

"I have to call home," you whisper as you creep around the room. "I don't see a phone! Where is the phone?"

"Calm down!" Terry replies. "We need to wait until Sombra comes back out and then demand some straight answers."

"Straight answers?" You hiss. "We don't know her. How can we trust her?"

"We don't know each *other*," Terry says. "But we have to rely on each other until we can sort this all out."

"I guess you're right," you reply as you rummage through the chest of the drawers. "We're in..."

You find a small, leather bag in one of the drawers. You open the bag and examine its contents – a bottle of ether, two small bottles of morphine, several syringes and needles, a roll of duct tape and a bundle of plastic, disposable restraints.

Your words seem to lodge in your throat, as if you have a rough-hewn stone stuck in your esophagus. "O...M...G!"

"What is it?" Terry inquires. "Jordan, what's wrong?"

"We have to get out of here," you gasp. "Look!"

You pull the bag from the drawer and toss it on the bed.

Terry peeks inside the bag. "What the...?"

"Exactly," you chime in. "Is Sombra saving us...or en*slaving* us? We should get out of here, now!"

"And go where?" Terry asks. "The police think we're murderers."

"We can go to the police ourselves," you answer. "Take that bag; convince them we were taken hostage by the *real* murderer."

"Are you serious?" Terry says, shaking her head. "Where did *you* grow up? You're African-American and I'm Afro-

Mexican – in the eyes of the police, we're guilty, until proven innocent."

"Well, we have to do *something*," you reply. "Either we make Sombra tell us everything – including why she has a bag full of knockout drugs and plastic handcuffs – or, we take the bag to the police as evidence and allow the courts to prove our innocence."

If you restrain Sombra and make her talk, go to page 117.

If you turn yourself – and Sombra's bag – in to the police, go to page 137.

"Stand right here," Jordan whispers, pointing to a spot on the floor about five feet in front of the bathroom door. "When she comes out, I'll push her toward you. You sweep her off of her feet with one of those cafeteria moves."

"Cafeteria?" You say, shaking your head." "It's Capoeira! And your plan sucks. I saw her fight. Her skills are *way* beyond mine."

"Trust me," Jordan says. "I can...see things; how events should go; where, when and how I should move."

"Yeah, I noticed that back at the Pyramid Arena," you reply. "It was like you knew where to run to avoid getting grabbed by those Henry dupes."

The bathroom door opens. Sombra steps out dressed in an indigo West African dress and head-wrap. She smiles at Jordan, who leans against the wall facing the bathroom door.

"You can go in now, Jordan," Sombra says as she walks by him.

Jordan slams his palms into Sombra's back, pushing with all his might.

Sombra stumbles toward you. You crouch low and then whip your right leg in a counterclockwise arc, tracing a semicircle on the floor with the inner edge of your foot.

Your right instep slams into Sombra's Achilles' tendon, just above her right heel.

Sombra's feet fly out from under her, but, to your surprise and dread, she somersaults over your head and lands, standing, behind you.

She turns to face you and Jordan, a slight smile upon her lips. "Nice try. Gonna try again?"

"Probably not," you reply.

"Don't," Sombra says. "You're a good person, I'd hate to kill you."

"*You're* a good person," you reply. "I'd hate to die."

Sombra laughs, which relieves some of your fear.

"Sit down," Sombra says, pointing toward a bed. "Both of you."

Jordan plops down on the bed.

You sit beside him. The bed has a

pleasant, woody scent.

"What are you planning to do to us?" Jordan asks, thrusting an accusing finger toward Sombra's doctor bag.

"It is my job to protect you," Sombra answers. "To deliver you to the Gatekeepers unscathed...well, alive, anyway."

"Then what's up with the bag?" You ask.

"Most people don't take the upheaval of their lives very well," Sombra replies. Most resist it. I don't have time for resistance."

"So, basically, you're kidnapping us," Jordan says.

"Basically, yes," Sombra says, smiling warmly.

"You say that so nicely and so cordially," you say.

"There is no rule that says when you do a kidnapping, you can't be nice and cordial," Sombra replies.

"You called us Keys earlier," Jordan says. "What are 'Keys' and why are they important?"

"Like I said," Sombra says. "You are the hosts of gods. Jordan, you are the avatar of the Igbo god of healing and divination, Agwu Nsi. Terry, you are the embodiment of the Aztec deity Cihuacoatl, a fierce warrior and leader of the spirits of women who die in childbirth – the fierce and feared Cihuateteo."

"Impossible," Jordan gasps.

"As impossible as your ability to see the path to the best choice," Sombra replies. "Or your superhuman five senses, Terry. And you both can do much more."

"Like control the weather, or stop time?" Jordan asks.

"Not even close," Sombra chuckles. "We never could have rendered a god with that kind of power dormant."

"What *can* we do, then?" You inquire.

"Rest up," Sombra says, sitting on the leather couch. "Tomorrow, your training will reveal all."

Sombra kicks her feet up onto the couch and lies back, resting her head on the arm of it.

"I won't be able to sleep," you say.

"I'm too nervous to sleep."

"Sure you will," Sombra says, closing her eyes. "I planted several vials of a concoction of iboga and muluga oil under each bed. When you sat down, you crushed a few vials."

"The woody scent," you sigh.

"Yep," Sombra replies. "You'll be out like a light in a minute or two.

Your vision blurs. A feeling of calm washes over you. You peer at Jordan, who is already asleep with a smile across his face. You yawn and then all goes black.

###

You awaken to the sweet smell of fruit – mango, watermelon, muscadine grapes – and spring water with fresh cucumber and lemon.

Sombra stands at the side of the bed, holding a bowl of fruit and a glass of water in which floats a slice of cucumber and lemon of course. "Eat and drink up. Your training begins in a half hour."

You peer over at Jordan, who is devouring the fruit.

You take the bowl and glass of water

from Sombra and eat. The delicious fruit and water give you energy, yet you are filled with a sublime serenity.

Probably still feeling the effects of Sombra's knockout concoction, you think.

After you and Jordan have finished the fruit and the water, Sombra leads you both out of the motel room. You follow her to the office. Sombra unlocks the door and pushes it open.

"Go past the desk and walk straight back," she says. "You'll see a door back there. It's unlocked; open it. You'll know what to do next."

You enter the office. Jordan follows you. Sombra steps back outside and closes the door. You hear the click of the door's lock.

"She locked us in," you sigh.

"Where is *she* going?" Jordan asks.

"I don't know," you answer. "But let's just do as she says and see what's behind that door."

"You're trusting her, now?" Jordan says, rolling his eyes.

"If she wanted to hurt us, she would

have done it while we were unconscious," you reply.

"That's true," Jordan sighs. "Okay, let's check out the door, but be ready to use that Cap-and-mirrors stuff."

"It's Capoeira," you say, shaking your head. "Cap-oh-*air*-uh; and I'm *always* ready."

"Alright, let's check it out, then," Jordan replies.

You walk past the dust-covered, old hardwood desk and creep toward the back of the office, which is dimly lit by a sliver of sun that cuts through a broken blind in the office door's window.

You reach the metal door at the back of the office. You push down on the door's handle and, as Sombra said, the door is unlocked. You pull it open

Before you is a landing and steps that appear to be carved from tan-hued limestone. The stairs descend into darkness.

You sniff the darkness. A smell akin to sweet incense rises from the darkness and kisses your nostrils.

You place your foot on the first step.

A torch on the wall ignites. This seems to cause a ripple effect as torch after torch ignites, one after another, revealing a winding staircase.

You saunter down the stairs. Jordan follows you.

Carved into the walls are depictions of warriors from different cultures fighting each other at the foot of pyramids.

"What *is* this place?" You whisper.

"I don't know, but it's creepy," Jordan replies.

You continue to descend the stairs. Your feet eventually leave the last step and land on something soft. You look down to find you are standing on sand.

You peruse the capacious room. It is about half the size of a football field and appears to be constructed of mahogany. The walls are inlaid with gold in the shape of strange runes. Lining the bottom edges of the walls are calabashes and clay pots of varying sizes. In the middle of the floor lie two large wooden rings and what appears to be a huge wooden sword. The room is illuminated by thousands of glowing, baseball-sized stones that dot the walls and ceiling.

"Whoa," Jordan gasps. "It looks like we stepped into a scene from a movie like *The Scythe* or *Amber and the Hidden City*!"

"Not quite," Sombra says, stepping out of the shadows in a far corner of the room. "You are standing in what the Oyo call *Ikole Orun* – the crossroads of spiritual and material; of darkness and light; of quick and dead. *This* is where we will bring forth the gods in you."

"And how long will that take?" You ask.

"As long as it takes," Sombra replies. "Two, maybe three years."

Jordan's eyes widen and his jaw falls slack. "Two or three *years*? My parents would lose their minds if I went missing for that long!"

"Not to worry," Sombra replies. "Time moves differently here. Two years in Ikole Orun are no more than two *days* on the terrestrial plane."

Sombra kneels before the weapons lying at the center of the floor. She picks up the pair of wooden rings, balancing them on her palms and forearms. She stands and saunters toward Jordan.

You notice that the rings are carved

in the shape of the ouroboros – the ancient symbol of the snake eating its tail.

Sombra extends her arms, thrusting the rings toward Jordan's chest. "These are the *itemo lindaa* – the ringed cudgels – preferred weapon of the ngamvulu, the great warriors of the Ateke people of Gabon; your maternal ancestors."

"My maternal ancestors are also Igbo," Jordan says.

"The pyramid builders," Sombra replies. "Yes, I know. They are the ancestors from whom you received your ability to see probabilities as patterns."

Jordan takes the rings from Sombra. He stares at them for a moment and then begins to swing the rings in a figure-eight pattern before him.

"That's it," Sombra says. "Feel them! Let the power of Agwu Nsi and your ancestors flow through and around you."

Jordan crouches low, holding the disc in his right hand before him, between his feet and the one in his left hand behind him, in line with the disc in his right hand. He explodes upward, leaping high into the air as he snaps his right hand upward and forward.

The itemo lindaa flies over Sombra's head and rockets across the room. The disc strikes the wall with a loud thud. It ricochets off the wall and then speeds back toward Sombra.

Jordan rolls past Sombra and then extends his right hand at the height of his brow.

The disc flies into Jordan's palm with a loud smack. Jordan closes his fingers around it and stands, staring wide-eyed at the disc in his hand.

"Your ability to see patterns will make you as formidable with the ringed cudgels as you are with a basketball," Sombra says.

"I assume that is mine," you say, pointing toward a flat, rectangular, sword-like weapon carved from umber-colored wood.

Sombra picks up the weapon. "The *macuahuitl* – carved from itin, one of the hardest woods in the world; its sides, embedded with razor sharp, prismatic blades, carved from obsidian – weapon of choice of the Aztec warrior elite."

Sombra hands the macuahuitl to you. The heavy weapon somehow feels *right* in your hands. Like it is a missing part of your very essence, returned.

"The Aztec warriors could use the flat side of the weapon as a club, to maim an opponent, or render him unconscious," Sombra says. "Or they could use the sharp edges to amputate limbs and decapitate heads."

Your body begins to feel very warm, as if a fire has been lit in the depths of your gut. The fire spreads to your limbs and coils up your spine. You feel that you must move; that you *must* wield the macuahuitl.

You cut the air with the weapon. It pulses in your hand. You hold the macuahuitl above your head and then somersault sideways. The weapon rends the air with a loud *whoosh.*

You land, kneeling, at Sombra's feet.

"Why did you perform the *au* –the somersault?" Sombra inquires.

"Because it felt right," you reply. "Like it was what the macuahuitl wanted me to do."

"Not the macuahuitl," Sombra says. "Cihuacoatl is awakening in you; guiding you. The macuahuitl is simply a tool to focus the power of Cihuacoatl, which seethes within you."

"It feels good," you say, feeling power cover you like a quilt in winter.

"Of course, it does," Sombra replies. "It always feels good to know yourself."

Sombra turns to her right and walks toward the wall. She stares at the runes as she speaks to you.

"Steel yourselves. What you are about to experience might seem impossible, but I assure you, it is quite real."

Sombra begins to chant something in a language you have never heard before. The room darkens; the thick, moist blackness swallowing the light of the torches.

The runes on the walls glow brightly, but the room remains black as pitch.

"Terry?" Jordan whispers.

"I'm here," you reply, struggling to keep your voice from shaking.

You sniff the air. You smell Jordan's fear. It is as strong as your own. You also smell something...else – a strange mix of grass, wisteria, urine and blood.

The strange smell grows stronger. Waves of nausea ebb and flow within your gut. You close your eyes and try to focus on something other than that horrible smell and the sick feeling bubbling in your belly.

Through your eyelids, you sense that light has returned to the room. Your nausea dissipates, as does the power of that revolting smell.

You open your eyes and find yourself standing in what appears to be a garden at the intersection of three footpaths. Within the garden are bushes that bear all manner of fruit. The sun breaks through the leaves of a massive old, oak tree, which is covered in purple wisteria.

Jordan stands beside you.

"Oh, my Goddess," you gasp.

"Apparently, you *are*," Jordan replies.

"I don't *feel* like a goddess," you say. "Right now, I just feel confused and scared out of my wits."

"Join the club," Jordan says.

"Well," you sigh, laying a gentle hand on Jordan's shoulder. "Which path do we take, smart boy?"

Jordan peruses his surroundings, gazing down each footpath. He shakes his head. "There isn't a best path to choose; we'll have to rely on those dog senses of *yours*, Scooby."

"Funny," you say, rolling your eyes.

You focus your hearing on the left path. You hear the clanking of metal and a hissing din, like the hissing of a gargantuan snake. You sniff the air, craning your head toward the path. The smell of smoke and steel hits you like a wrecking ball.

You withdraw your focus and target your senses on the center path. The pleasant scent of freshly cut grass and roses and the sound of a gentle breeze greet you. Under the calming whistle of the breeze, however, is a faint panting, like a large dog in need of water after a run.

The right path smells like river water and feces. A loud croaking, like a symphony of a thousand frogs, assaults your ears.

"So," Jordan begins. "Which path is it going to be?"

If you take the left path, go to page 141.

If you take the center path, go to page 197.

If you take the right path, go to page 168.

"Stand right here," you whisper, pointing to a spot on the floor about five feet in front of the bathroom door. "When she comes out, I'll push her toward you. You sweep her off of her feet with one of those cafeteria moves."

"Cafeteria?" She says, shaking her head." "It's Capoeira! And your plan sucks. I saw Sombra fight. Her skills are *way* beyond mine."

"Trust me," you reply. "I can...see things; how events should go; where, when and how I should move."

"Yeah, I noticed that back at the Pyramid Arena," Terry replies. "It was like you knew where to run to avoid getting grabbed by those Henry dupes."

The bathroom door opens. Sombra steps out dressed in an indigo West African dress and head-wrap. She smiles at you.

"You can go in now, Jordan," Sombra says as she walks by you.

You inhale deeply, gathering your nerve and then slam your palms into Sombra's back, pushing with all your might.

Sombra stumbles toward Terry.

Terry crouches low and then whips her right leg in a counterclockwise arc, tracing a semicircle on the floor with the inner edge of her foot.

Her right instep slams into Sombra's Achilles' tendon, just above her right heel.

Sombra's feet fly out from under her, but, to your surprise and dread, she somersaults over Terry's head and lands, standing, behind her.

She turns to face you and Terry, a slight smile upon her lips. "Nice try. Gonna try again?"

"Probably not," Terry replies.

"Don't," Sombra says. "You're a good person; I'd hate to kill you."

"*You're* a good person," Terry replies. "I'd hate to die."

Sombra laughs, which relieves some of your fear.

"Sit down," Sombra says, pointing toward a bed. "Both of you."

You plop down on the bed, relieved Sombra didn't beat you to a pulp.

Terry sits beside you.

"What are you planning to do to us?" you ask, thrusting an accusing finger toward Sombra's doctor bag.

"It is my job to protect you," Sombra answers. "To deliver you to the Gatekeepers unscathed...well, alive, anyway."

"Then what's up with the bag?" Terry asks.

"Most people don't take the upheaval of their lives very well," Sombra replies. Most resist it. I don't have time for resistance."

"So, basically, you're kidnapping us," you say.

"Basically, yes," Sombra says, smiling warmly.

"You say that so nicely and so cordially," Terry says, frowning.

"There is no rule that says when you do a kidnapping, you can't be nice and cordial," Sombra replies.

"You called us Keys earlier," you say. "What are 'Keys' and why are they important?"

"Like I said," Sombra says. "You are

the hosts of gods. Jordan, you are the avatar of the Igbo god of healing and divination, Agwu Nsi. Terry, you are the embodiment of the Aztec deity Cihuacoatl, a fierce warrior and leader of the spirits of women who die in childbirth, the fierce and feared Cihuateteo."

"Impossible," you gasp.

"As impossible as your ability to see the path to the best choice," Sombra replies. "Or your superhuman five senses, Terry. And you both can do much more."

Wow! If this lady isn't totally nuts, I might become a real costumed avenger, you think. *The first superhero in the world!*

"Like control the weather, or stop time?" you ask.

"Not even close," Sombra chuckles. "We never could have rendered a god with that kind of power dormant."

"What *can* we do, then?" Terry inquires.

"Rest up," Sombra says, sitting on the leather couch. "Tomorrow, your training will reveal all."

Sombra kicks her feet up onto the couch and lies back, resting her head on the arm of it.

"I won't be able to sleep," Terry says. "I'm too nervous to sleep."

"Sure you will," Sombra says, closing her eyes. "I planted several vials of a concoction of iboga and muluga oil under each bed. When you sat down, you crushed a few vials."

Your vision blurs. A feeling of calm washes over you. You yawn and then all goes black.

You awaken to the sweet smell of sweet fruit.

Sombra stands at the side of the bed, holding a bowl of fruit and a glass of water in which floats a slice of cucumber and a lemon. "Eat and drink up. Your training begins in forty minutes."

You take the bowl and glass from Sombra. The delicious fruit and water give you energy, yet you are filled with a sublime serenity.

"Where did you buy this fruit?" You ask. It has me feeling all serene and what not."

"That feeling is from the effects of my sleep concoction," Sombra says. "Now eat up while I rouse Terry. We have much work to do."

Sombra awakens Terry, who rises and devours her breakfast.

After you and Terry have finished the fruit and the water, Sombra leads you both out of the motel room. You follow her to the office. Sombra unlocks the door and pushes it open.

"Go past the desk and walk straight back," she says. "You'll see a door back there. It's unlocked; open it. You'll know what to do next."

Terry enters the office. You follow her. Sombra steps back outside and closes the door. You hear the click of the door's lock.

"She locked us in," Terry sighs.

"Where is *she* going?" you ask.

"I don't know," Terry answers. "But let's just do as she says and see what's behind that door."

"You're trusting her, now?" you say, rolling your eyes.

"If she wanted to hurt us, she would have done it while we were unconscious," Terry replies.

I guess she's right, you think.

"That's true," you sigh. "Okay, let's check out the door, but be ready to use that Cap-and-mirrors stuff."

"It's Capoeira," Terry says, shaking her head. "Cap-oh-*air*-uh; and I'm *always* ready."

You turn away from Terry and fight a smile from spreading across your face. It is fun misnaming the martial art she is so passionate about and seeing how it drives her nuts.

"Alright, let's check it out, then," you reply, turning back to face Terry.

You walk past the dust-covered, old hardwood desk and creep toward the back of the office, which is dimly lit by a sliver of sun that cuts through a broken blind in the office door's window.

You reach the metal door at the back of the office.

Terry pushes down on the door's handle and, as Sombra said, the door is unlocked. She pulls it open

Before you is a landing and steps that appear to be carved from tan-hued limestone. The stairs descend into darkness.

Terry places her foot on the first step. A torch on the wall ignites. This seems to cause a ripple effect as torch after torch ignites, one after another, revealing a winding staircase.

You and Terry saunter down the stairs.

Carved into the walls are depictions of warriors from different cultures fighting each other at the foot of pyramids.

"What *is* this place?" Terry whispers.

"I don't know, but it's creepy," you reply.

You continue to descend the stairs. Your feet eventually leave the last step and land on something soft. You look down to find you are standing on sand.

You peruse the capacious room. It is about half the size of a football field and appears to be constructed of mahogany. The walls are inlaid with gold in the shape of strange runes. Lining the bottom edges of the walls are calabashes and clay pots of varying sizes. In the middle of the floor lie two large wooden rings and what appears to be a huge wooden sword. The room is illuminated by thousands of glowing, baseball-sized stones that dot the walls and ceiling.

"Whoa," you gasp. "It looks like we stepped into a scene from a movie like *The Scythe* or *Amber and the Hidden City*!"

"Not quite," Sombra says, stepping out of the shadows in a far corner of the room. "You are standing in what the Oyo call *Ikole Orun* – the crossroads of spiritual and material; of darkness and light; of quick and dead. *This* is where we will bring forth the gods in you."

"And how long will that take?" Terry asks.

"As long as it takes," Sombra replies. "Two, maybe three years."

Sombra's words hit you like a smack in the face. You cannot spend three *nights* away from your warm bed, some hot pizza and even hotter girls, let alone three *years*!

"Two or three *years*?" You cry. "My parents would lose their minds if I went missing for that long!"

"Not to worry," Sombra replies.

"Time moves differently here. Two years in Ikole Orun are no more than two *days* on the terrestrial plane."

Sombra kneels before the weapons lying at the center of the floor. She picks up the pair of wooden rings, balancing them on her palms and forearms. She stands and saunters toward you.

You notice that the rings are carved in the shape of the ouroboros – the ancient symbol of the snake eating its tail.

Sombra extends her arms, thrusting the rings toward your chest. The rings are carved in the shape of a snake eating its tail.

"These are the *itemo lindaa* – the ringed cudgels – preferred weapon of the ngamvulu, the great warriors of the Ateke people of Gabon," Sombra says. Your maternal ancestors."

"My maternal ancestors are also Igbo," you say.

"The pyramid builders," Sombra replies. "Yes, I know. They are the ancestors from whom you received your ability to see probabilities as patterns."

You take the rings from Sombra. You stare at them for a moment. Your body begins to feel very warm, as if a fire has been lit in the depths of your gut. The fire spreads to your limbs and coils up your spine. You feel that you must move; that you *must* wield the itemo lindaa. You begin swinging the rings in a figure-eight pattern before you.

"That's it," Sombra says. "Feel them! Let the power of Agwu Nsi and your ancestors flow through and around you."

You crouch low, holding the disc in your right hand before him, between your feet and the one in your left hand behind you, in line with the disc in your right hand. You explode upward, leaping high into the air as you snap your right hand upward and forward.

The itemo lindaa flies over Sombra's head and rockets across the room. The disc strikes the wall with a loud thud. It ricochets off the wall and then speeds back toward Sombra.

You roll past Sombra and then extend your right hand at the height of your brow.

The disc flies into your palm with a loud smack, but you don't feel any pain. In fact, it feels like a 'high-five' from an overzealous teammate after you score the winning point in a game.

You close your fingers around the weapon and stand, staring wide-eyed at the disc. It pulses in your hand.

How did I know how to throw it? You wonder. *To catch it with ease?*

"Your ability to see patterns will make you as formidable with the ringed cudgels as you are with a basketball," Sombra says.

"I assume that is mine," Terry says, pointing toward a flat, rectangular, sword-like weapon carved from umber-colored wood.

Sombra picks up the weapon. "The *macuahuitl* – carved from itin, one of the hardest woods in the world; its sides, embedded with razor sharp, prismatic blades, carved from obsidian – weapon of choice of the Aztec warrior elite."

Sombra hands the macuahuitl to Terry.

"The Aztec warriors could use the flat side of the weapon as a club, to maim an opponent, or render him unconscious," Sombra says. "Or they could use the sharp edges to amputate limbs and decapitate heads."

Terry cuts the air with the weapon. She holds the macuahuitl above her head and then somersaults sideways. The weapon rends the air with a loud *whoosh.*

Terry lands, kneeling, at Sombra's feet.

"Why did you perform the *au* –the somersault?" Sombra inquires.

"Because it felt right," Terry replies. "Like it was what the macuahuitl wanted me to do."

"Not the macuahuitl," Sombra says. "Cihuacoatl is awakening in you; guiding you. The macuahuitl is simply a tool to focus the power of Cihuacoatl, which seethes within you."

"It feels good," Terry says.

"Of course, it does," Sombra replies. "It always feels good to know yourself."

Sombra turns to her right and walks toward the wall. She stares at the runes as she speaks to you.

"Steel yourselves. What you are about to experience might seem impossible, but I assure you, it is quite real."

Sombra begins to chant something in a language you have never heard before. The room darkens; the thick, moist blackness swallowing the light of the torches.

The runes on the walls glow brightly, but the room remains black as pitch.

The darkness is somehow terrifying. You feel alone in its all consuming blackness.

"Terry?" you whisper.

"I'm here," she replies, her voice a bit shaky.

The darkness seems to last a lifetime then, suddenly, it fades, giving way to sunlight.

You find yourself standing in what appears to be a garden at the intersection of three footpaths. Within the garden are bushes that bear all manner of fruit. The sun breaks through the leaves of a massive old, oak tree, which is covered in purple wisteria.

Terry stands beside you. Her face is pallid and sweat runs down her cheeks.

"Oh, my Goddess," she gasps.

"Apparently, you *are*," you reply, struggling to hide your nervousness.

"I don't *feel* like a goddess," Terry says. "Right now, I just feel confused and scared out of my wits."

"Join the club," you sigh.

"Well," Terry says, laying a soft hand on your shoulder. "Which path do we take, smart boy?"

You peruse your surroundings, gazing down each footpath. A red line is visible on each path. No line is more brilliant than the other.

"There isn't a best path to choose," you say, shaking your head. "We'll have to rely on those dog senses of *yours*, Scooby."

"Funny," Terry says, rolling her eyes.

She cranes her head toward the path on the left, sniffing the air. A moment later, she shakes her head.

She then focuses on the center path, but shakes her head again.

She focuses on the right path. A second later, she turns up her nose and shakes her head a final time.

Well, you think. *I guess the choice is* mine.

If you take the left path, go to page 152.

If you take the center path, go to page 212.

If you take the right path, go to page 183.

"We should just take the bag to the police," Jordan says. "With the bag as evidence, we can just tell the police that we were kidnapped and *forced* to do whatever they are accusing us of."

"They're accusing us of murder," you reply with a smirk. "As in we killed somebody; as in we get life imprisonment or the death penalty; as in adios...sayonara...buh-bye; as in..."

"Ok, I get it," Jordan says. "Well, our only other option is to subdue Sombra and make her tell us – or the authorities – exactly what she's up to. You've seen her fight; do you think the two of us can take her down?"

"Nope," you sigh. "I don't trust the police as far as I can throw them, but I guess we don't have any other option except to turn ourselves – and that bag – in."

Jordan creeps toward the door. "Come on!"

You follow him.

Jordan tries to open the door. It does not budge. "What the...? We're locked in, somehow!"

You kneel down, inspecting the door

knob. It has a simple knob lock. You peer at the door jamb, inspecting its bolt lock. You notice that it has a double bolt-lock mechanism.

"This door requires a key to unlock the bolt–lock from the inside *and* the outside," you sigh. Sombra must have locked it when we weren't paying attention."

"We go out the window, then," Jordan says, frowning.

He grabs the chair and lifts it high above his head.

You snatch the curtain toward you, exposing the large stationary window. You then scurry backward, away from the window, just as Jordan hurls the chair.

The chair hits the window with a dull thud and then falls to the floor. The glass is unscathed.

"It's bulletproof."

You turn toward the voice.

Sombra stands before you. She draws a wicked-looking, curved knife from the folds of her head-wrap.

"The Gatekeepers said you were the

Keys," Sombra says. "I disagreed. I told them that the world isn't ready for the power the pyramids grant us. Man is filled with too much hatred; too much fear; too much disharmony and distrust."

Sombra takes a step forward, brandishing the knife before her chest. "You are not the Keys; your actions prove that."

Your throat feels as if a jagged stone is lodged in it. Sweat beads on your forehead and your pulse pounds.

"Umm, s-so you might as well let us l-leave, so you can find the *real* Keys, r-right?" Jordan stutters.

"Unfortunately, you know too much," Sombra replies. "I cannot allow you to live. I am truly sorry."

The last thing you see is Sombra charging toward you and the flash of steel before your eyes.

The End

"We should just take the bag to the police," you say. "With the bag as evidence, we can just tell the police that we were kidnapped and *forced* to do whatever they are accusing us of."

"They're accusing us of murder," Terry replies with a smirk. "As in we killed somebody; as in we get life imprisonment or the death penalty; as in adios...sayonara...buh-bye; as in..."

There she goes with that smart mouth, again, you think. *She's just acting like this to mask her fear. Well, here's my chance to be her hero.*

"Ok, I get it," you say. "Well, our only other option is to subdue Sombra and make her tell us – or the authorities – exactly what she's up to. You've seen her fight; do you think the two of us can take her down?"

"Nope," Terry sighs. "I don't trust the police as far as I can throw them, but I guess we don't have any other option except to turn ourselves – and that bag – in."

You creep toward the door. "Come on!"

Terry follows you.

You try to open the door. It does not budge. "What the...? We're locked in, somehow!"

Terry kneels down, inspecting the door knob. She then inspects the door jamb.

Terry looks up at you. Her face is a mask of worry. "This door requires a key to unlock the bolt–lock from the inside *and* the outside. Sombra must have locked it when we weren't paying attention."

"We go out the window, then," you say, hiding your fear behind a frown.

You grab the chair and lift it high above your head.

Terry follows your lead and snatches the curtain back, exposing the large stationary window. She scurries backward, making way for your assault on the window.

You hurl the chair. It hits the window with a dull thud and then falls to the floor. The glass is unscathed.

"It's bulletproof."

You whirl toward the voice.

Sombra stands before you. She

draws a wicked-looking, curved knife from the folds of her head-wrap..

"The Gatekeepers said you were the Keys," Sombra says. "I disagreed. I told them that the world isn't ready for the power the pyramids grant us. Man is filled with too much hatred; too much fear; too much disharmony and distrust."

Sombra takes a step forward, brandishing the knife before her chest. "You are not the Keys; your actions prove that."

Fear sweeps over you like a tempest.

"Umm, s-so you might as well let us l-leave, so you can find the *real* Keys, r-right?" you stutter.

"Unfortunately, you know too much," Sombra replies. "I cannot allow you to live. I am truly sorry."

The last thing you see is Sombra charging toward you and the flash of steel before your eyes.

The End

"I feel uneasy about each path," you say. "But there is a clanking noise down the left path and the smell of smoke, which might indicate a factory of some kind. And where there's a factory..."

"There's people," Jordan chimes in.

"Follow me," you say, pointing your macuahuitl down the path.

Jordan follows closely behind you as you creep down the winding footpath.

After about a half mile of marching, the grass beneath your feet gives way to cobblestone. A pillar of white smoke rises in the distance. The sound of clanking metal grows louder; closer.

You sniff the air.

"That sound isn't coming from a factory," you say. "It's coming from..."

"A train!" Jordan shouts, pointing at an old steam train that speeds toward you.

"Yeah," you reply. "But how is that train running? There's no track!"

The train's wheels kick up grass and dirt as they slice through the soft, red earth. The train slows, coming to a screeching stop a few yards away from you.

The locomotive is massive – much larger than any you have seen in pictures or on television. You figure it stands at a height of nearly twenty feet and pulls a train of cars that stretch half the length of a football field.

"Hello?" You shout. "Who's on board?"

No one answers.

"Hello?" You say again.

Still, no answer.

"I don't like this," Jordan whispers.

A shrill, whistling din erupts from the train.

You press your palms to your ears to block out the noise.

"What's happening?" Jordan asks.

"I don't know," you reply. "Just be ready."

"Ready for what?" Jordan asks.

"For anything," you say.

The locomotive's rods and pistons partially dislodge from its frame. The locomotive hisses and a cloud of steam pours out of it in dense white waves.

The steam thickens, engulfing the locomotive in what looks, to you, like some form of cocoon. The steam cocoon pulses like the beating of an aged heart.

"I think we should go now," Jordan says.

"I think so, too," you reply. "Let's take the center path instead."

You turn back toward the path.

"Oh no," you gasp.

The cobblestone path is gone, replaced by a row of Victorian-style shops, a saloon, a brothel and a hotel.

"Where did *that* come from?" Jordan asks.

"Heck if I know," you reply.

You spot a man step out of one of the shops in the distance.

"Maybe he can tell us," Jordan says, pointing at the man.

The man's face is concealed by a top

hat, but there is something familiar about the way he moves; about his lean silhouette. You sniff the air. You smell steam and sawdust and…juniper.

"Jordan, that's Henry the Navigator!" You say.

"Oh, my God," Jordan says. "What do we do?"

"We fight!" You reply, raising your macuahuitl to the height of your chest.

Henry the Navigator saunters toward a carriage that sits across the dirt road directly opposite him. He climbs into it. A moment later, one of Henry's gray-clad duplicates climbs out of the carriage and into the driver's seat. He snaps the reins and the twin horses tethered to the carriage trot up the road toward you, pulling Henry's red oak carriage with them.

Henry's duplicate brings the horses to a stop less than a yard from you.

The carriage door opens.

Jordan brings the itemo lindaa in his left hand to his right shoulder and the one in his right hand to the side of his head, in line with his right ear.

You crouch low, pointing your macuahuitl at the carriage.

One of Henry's duplicates creeps out of the carriage, stepping gingerly onto the dirt road. Another duplicate steps out of the carriage and the third leaps down from the driver's seat.

The three gray-clad men line up, shoulder-to-shoulder, standing tall and at attention.

Henry the Navigator steps out of the carriage and stands behind the trio. He peers over the middle duplicate's shoulder, grinning.

"Good morning Jordan; Terry," he says. "Have you come to join me as friends, or die as enemies?"

"Where are we?" You ask, ignoring Henry's question.

"The more salient question is *when* are you?" Henry replies, still grinning. "The answer to that would be 1834."

"1830-whatsis?" Jordan shouts.

"1834," Henry says again. "May 11, 1843, to be exact."

"And we're in the Wild West, I

assume," you say.

"The Wild *South*," Henry replies. "Marthasville, Georgia, originally called Terminus. Not a safe place for people of your hue. You'd be wise to come with me."

"Umm...no," you say, shaking your head. "My mama warned me to stay away from dudes who speak with booboo-eating grins on their faces."

"And you, Jordan?" Henry asks.

"I'm with *her*," Jordan replies, tilting his head toward you. "She's *waaay* hotter than you and not, you know, *creepy*. You've got a better manicure, though."

Henry's smile fades. His duplicates step backward, the heels of their shoes melting into his shins. Inch by inch, the duplicates fold into Henry's flesh with a wet, sucking noise until only Henry stands before you.

"You both think that you are so funny," Henry hisses.

His smile returns. "Let's see what jokes you have for Loco."

"Loco?" Jordan snickers. "You mean *you* aren't loco enough?"

Henry takes a few steps backward, closes his eyes and inhales deeply.

A whirring, hissing noise erupts behind you.

You and Jordan spin on your heels, toward the source of the noise, almost simultaneously.

"Oh, snap!" Jordan gasps, staring, wide-eyed at what lay before him. "I guess *that's* Loco."

Rising out of the torn "steam cocoon" is a creature that can only be described as a monstrous, iron kangaroo. Its head, formed from the cabin of the locomotive is small in relation to the huge iron body and where its ears should be stand two iron chimneys. Its thick legs are comprised of the train's wheels, rods and pistons; its feet and tail forged from the rail cars and its torso is constructed from the locomotive's smoke-box. Instead of a pouch, a circular, hinged, iron door – once belonging to the smoke-box – sits upon the monster's belly.

Loco roars, belching a thick cloud of black smoke. Steam billows out of its chimney ears.

The creature leaps high into the air,

momentarily holding itself aloft with its massive tail. It then plunges, feet first, toward you.

Jordan rolls backward. You somersault sideways to evade the kangaroo's boxcar feet.

Loco lands with a loud crash. The ground collapses half a foot beneath its bulk.

You swing the macuahuitl at Loco's left leg, fully expecting the wood and obsidian weapon to break against Loco's ferrous hide, but you know that you must do *something*.

To your surprise, the macuahuitl does not break. Sparks fly from Loco's leg, accompanied by staccato blasts of steam.

A metallic howl rises from Loco's mouth. Two gusts of black smoke surge the monster's chimneys.

You hear an agonized wail behind you. You peer over your shoulder. Henry the Navigator has collapsed onto one knee.

They're connected somehow, you think. *Loco and Henry. Just like Henry and his dupes. You hurt Henry's creations, you hurt him!*

You turn toward Jordan to tell him, but he has already hurled both of his throwing cudgels at Henry and is sprinting toward the creep.

One ring-shaped cudgel slams into Henry's gut with a dull thud.

Henry gasps as the force of the cudgel sends him reeling backward.

The second cudgel crashes into Henry's left knee.

Henry screams. His knee bends backward at a sickening angle. Henry collapses onto his haunches.

Rods and gears fly from Loco's left leg. The limb buckles, quivers and then spits puffs of steam in protest.

"Hurt Loco, you hurt Henry," you call out to Jordan.

"Hurt *Henry*, you hurt *Loco*," Jordan calls back.

A noise, like metal grinding against, metal assaults your ears. You snap your head toward the sound and find Loco's boxcar tail speeding toward you. The iron appendage hammers into your chest.

You feel the air rush from your

lungs and taste blood in your mouth. Your limp body is sent careening through the air. You somehow maintain your grip on your macuahuitl but your arm will not follow your brain's command to raise the weapon.

If it wasn't for the power of Cihuacoatl, that blow would have killed me instantly, you think. *If only my arms would work...I'd kill that monster and Henry, too.*

You sail past Jordan, who stands over a bleeding Henry, set to deliver a blow to the Navigator's head.

As your vision fades, you hope, beyond hope, that Jordan defeats Henry and doesn't die trying, like you.

The End

"I feel uneasy about each path," Terry says. "But there is a clanking noise down the left path and the smell of smoke, which might indicate a factory of some kind. And where there's a factory..."

"There are people," you chime in.

"Follow me," Terry says, pointing your macuahuitl down the path.

You follow closely behind her as she creeps down the winding footpath.

After about a half mile of marching, the grass beneath your feet gives way to cobblestone. A pillar of white smoke rises in the distance. The sound of clanking metal grows louder; closer.

Terry sniffs the air.

"That sound isn't coming from a factory," she says. "It's coming from..."

You spot an odd scene in the distance – an old steam train speeding toward you.

"A train!" You shout, pointing at it.

"Yeah," Terry replies. "But how is that train running? There's no track!"

The train's wheels kick up grass and dirt as they slice through the soft, red earth. The train slows, coming to a screeching stop a few yards away from you.

The locomotive is massive – much larger than any you have seen in pictures or on television. You figure it stands at a height of nearly twenty feet and pulls a train of cars that stretch half the length of a football field.

"Hello?" Terry shouts. "Who's on board?"

No one answers.

"Hello?" She says again.

Still, no answer.

"I don't like this," you whisper.

A whistling din erupts from the train.

You press your palms to your ears to block out the noise.

"What's happening?" you shout above the shrill noise.

"I don't know," Terry replies. "Just be ready."

"Ready for what?" you ask.

"For anything," she says.

The locomotive's rods and pistons partially dislodge from its frame. The locomotive hisses and a cloud of steam pours out of it in dense white waves.

The steam thickens, engulfing the locomotive in what looks, to you, like some form of cocoon. The steam cocoon pulses like the beating of an aged heart.

"I think we should go now," you say, backing away from the cocoon.

"I think so, too," Terry replies. "Let's take the center path instead."

You turn back toward the path.

"Oh no," Terry gasps.

The cobblestone path is gone, replaced by a row of Victorian-style shops, a saloon, a brothel and a hotel.

"Where did *that* come from?" you inquire.

"Heck if I know," Terry replies.

You spot the silhouette of a man step out of one of the shops in the distance.

"Maybe he can tell us," you say,

pointing at the silhouette.

Terry squints, staring at the man. She then sniffs the air. Her eyes grow wide. She stares at you, trembling.

"Jordan, that's Henry the Navigator!" She says.

Sweat forms on your forehead and runs, in rivers, down your brow. "Oh, my God! What do we do?"

"We fight!" Terry replies, raising her macuahuitl to the height of her chest.

Terry is just like Lala, from the Redeemer graphic novel, you think. *Crazy and always ready for a fight. She's just as hot, too!* One day, you'll let Terry read the book and tell her just that...if you live through this.

Henry the Navigator saunters toward a carriage that sits across the dirt road directly opposite him. He climbs into it. A moment later, one of his gray-clad duplicates climbs out of the carriage and into the driver's seat. He snaps the reins and the twin horses tethered to the carriage trot up the road toward you, pulling Henry's red oak carriage with them.

Henry's duplicate brings the horses

to a stop less than a yard from you.

The carriage door opens.

Welp...time to throw down, you think.

You bring the itemo lindaa in your left hand to your right shoulder and the one in your right hand to the side of your head, in line with your right ear.

Terry crouches low, pointing her macuahuitl at the carriage.

One of Henry's duplicates creeps out of the carriage, stepping gingerly onto the dirt road. Another duplicate steps out of the carriage and the third leaps down from the driver's seat.

The three gray-clad men line up, shoulder-to-shoulder, standing tall and at attention.

Henry the Navigator steps out of the carriage and stands behind the trio. He peers over the middle duplicate's shoulder, grinning.

"Good morning Jordan; Terry," he says. "Have you come to join me as friends, or die as enemies?"

"Where are we?" Terry asks.

"The more salient question is *when* are you?" Henry replies, still grinning. "The answer to that would be 1834."

"1830-whatsis?" you shout.

"1834," Henry says again. "May 11, 1843, to be exact."

"And we're in the Wild West, I assume," Terry says.

"The Wild *South*," Henry replies. "Marthasville, Georgia, originally called Terminus. Not a safe place for people of your hue. You'd be wise to come with me."

"Umm...no," Terry replies, shaking her head. "My mama warned me to stay away from dudes who speak with booboo-eating grins on their faces."

"And you, Jordan?" Henry asks.

"I'm with *her*," you reply, tilting your head toward Terry. "She's *waaay* hotter than you and not, you know, *creepy*. You've got a better manicure, though."

Henry's smile fades. His duplicates step backward, the heels of their shoes melting into his shins. Inch by inch, the duplicates fold into Henry's flesh with a wet, sucking noise until only Henry stands before you.

"You both think that you are so funny," Henry hisses.

His smile returns. "Let's see what jokes you have for Loco."

"Loco?" You snicker. You hope that your taunts will anger Henry enough to leave an opening you can take advantage of, just like you do to your opponents on the basketball court. "You mean *you* aren't loco enough?"

Henry takes a few steps backward, closes his eyes and inhales deeply.

A whirring, hissing noise erupts behind you.

You and Terry spin on your heels, toward the source of the noise, almost simultaneously.

"Oh, snap!" you gasp, staring, wide-eyed at what lay before you. "I guess *that's* Loco."

Rising out of the torn "steam cocoon" is a creature that can only be described as a monstrous, iron kangaroo. Its head, formed from the cabin of the locomotive is small in relation to the huge iron body and where its ears should be stand two iron chimneys. Its thick legs are comprised of the train's wheels, rods and pistons; its feet and tail forged from the rail cars and its torso is constructed from the locomotive's smoke-box. Instead of a pouch, a circular, hinged, iron door – once belonging to the smoke-box – sits upon the monster's belly.

Loco roars, belching a thick cloud of black smoke. Steam billows out of its chimney ears.

The creature leaps high into the air, momentarily holding itself aloft with its massive tail. It then plunges, feet first, toward you.

Terry somersaults sideways. You roll backward, just barely evading the kangaroo's boxcar feet.

Loco lands with a loud crash. The ground collapses half a foot beneath its bulk.

You hop up onto your feet and look around for Terry, hoping that she has not been crushed under Loco's terrible weight.

You spot her. She boldly attacks Loco with her macuahuitl, slashing desperately at the giant's left leg.

Steam erupts from a gaping wound in Loco's left ankle. The iron monstrosity lets loose a whistling howl, vomiting black smoke into the air from its chimney ears.

Out of the corner of your eye, you see something move. You snap your head toward the movement. Henry the Navigator collapses onto his left knee, wailing in pain.

Henry feels the same pain as Loco, you think. *Just like his duplicates. So, if I hurt Henry, will Loco feel it?*

You inhale deeply and focus on Henry. Two glowing, crimson lines appear before you, extending from your feet to Henry. One line ends at Henry's abdomen, the other, a few inches lower.

You hurl the pair of itemo lindaa. The throwing cudgels fly along the path of the glowing, red lines, whistling as they carve the air around them.

You close on Henry, sprinting behind your weapons.

The first cudgel strikes Henry in the gut, lifting him off his feet. Henry staggers backward. A line of spittle runs from the corner of his mouth and down his cheek.

The second itemo lindaa slams into Henry's knee.

Henry screams. His knee bends

backward with a loud pop and then collapses inward at a sickening angle. Henry slumps onto his haunches.

The itemo lindaa fly back toward you. You catch them in mid-stride as you continue to run toward the injured Henry.

"Hurt Loco, you hurt Henry!" You hear Terry shout.

You peer over your shoulder at her. Terry stands over Loco. The iron kangaroo has collapsed onto its left leg.

"Hurt Henry, you hurt Loco!" You shout back.

You now stand over Henry. He looks up at you, his face twisted into a mask of fear and rage.

You raise your right hand above your head and then bring it down forcefully, hammering the bridge of Henry's nose with the cudgel.

Henry's head snaps backward. Blood flies into the air and then lands, in a spider web pattern, on Henry's face.

You raise your left hand, ready to strike again.

The sound of crashing metal gives

you pause. A moment later, Terry's limp body sails past you. Her face looks pained. Her arms flop loosely at her sides. Somehow, though, she continues to tightly grip her weapon.

Terry lands a few yards away from you. She convulses once and then lies still.

No!" You scream.

"Yes," Henry hisses. "Oh, yes! You should have accepted my offer, boy. If you had, your girlfriend would still be alive and you wouldn't be about to die!"

A duplicate's head slithers out of Henry's chest. Another peeks out from his shoulder.

You hear the pounding of Loco's footsteps drawing near.

You whirl toward Loco, flicking both wrists. The itemo lindaa fly from your hands and speed toward the giant.

Loco raises its arm, swatting away the first cudgel like a bothersome gnat. The weapon flies high into the sky, disappearing, seemingly, into the clouds.

The second itemo lindaa gets past Loco's cumbersome defense, however. The cudgel strikes the center of Loco's neck, where a man's Adam's apple would be located.

The creature vomits a pillar of steam and then collapses onto its haunches.

Henry grasps his throat. A strange, croaking din slithers from between his flaccid lips. The duplicates retreat back into their host.

The itemo lindaa ricochets off of Loco's neck and flies back toward your open palm. You strike Henry across the jaw with it.

Henry's chin tilts off-center. He spits a wad of blood at your feet. "Is that all you got, boy?"

"Nope," you reply, slamming the back of your open left hand onto Henry's forehead. Your knuckles bruise Henry's pale flesh. You grind your knuckles into Henry's forehead.

Henry laughs. "A backhanded slap to my forehead? Really? You *do* have much to learn!"

Suddenly, the itemo lindaa appears from the clouds. It plummets at a tremendous speed toward you. Toward your open, left palm.

Right before the itemo lindaa touches your palm, you snatch your hand away.

"No!" Henry screams, realizing his predicament.

The cudgel crashes into Henry's skull. It slices through his forehead and then skips along the ground behind him.

The top of Henry's head tumbles down his back and then rolls a few feet behind him, leaving a trail of pinkish-gray flesh.

Henry falls onto his face.

Loco falls onto *its* face.

Neither monster moves again.

You run toward Terry but she – and the world around you – fade, giving way to darkness.

A moment later, you find yourself back in the room with the strange runes beneath the motel.

Sombra stands before you, smiling. "You made it!"

She cranes her neck, peeking around you. "Where's Terry?"

You feel heat rising up the back of your neck and anger rising with it.

"Gone, thanks to you!" You reply. "You sent us to that crazy place to die!"

"I sent you to become who you were destined to be," Sombra says. "I thought you would be gone much longer; you were gone but a moment – less than four breaths. There is much more for you to do."

"I killed Henry," you say. "What more *is* there?"

"You killed him in one realm of existence," Sombra replies. "So, another duplicate is dead, but Henry's spirit lives on in *this* world."

"Then, let's find him and end him, once and for all!" You shout.

"I know you want to avenge Terry's death," Sombra says. "And you'll have your chance, but right now, we must find the next Key. There must be two of you."

"The *next* Key?" You inquire. "How many of us *are* there?"

"Not many," Sombra replies. "Three; perhaps four. There is one other I have been keeping an eye on. Now, let's go.

Time is of the essence."

If you go with Sombra in search of the new Key, go to page 227.

If you refuse to go with Sombra, go to page 229.

"There's a weird croaking noise coming from the right path," you say. "But I smell a river. Maybe we can follow it to a place where people are nearby and they can tell us where we are."

"Maybe," Jordan replies. "But what's that croaking?" Frogs?

"If it *is* frogs, there must be thousands of them," you say. "They're *loud*. Oh, I also smell blood."

"Animal? Human?" Jordan asks.

"I don't know."

"Well, only one way to find out," Jordan says, tracing a wide arc in the air with his arm and pointing his fingers down the footpath. "After you, milady."

You hold your weapon chest-high and step onto the path. Jordan follows a few paces behind you.

"Best view ever!" He says.

You peer over your shoulder. Jordan is staring at your backside with a broad smile stretched across his face.

You roll your eyes. "Try not to act like a ten year old, okay?"

"There is no try," Jordan replies.

"Only do or don't."

"Then, *do*," you say.

"I'll try," Jordan replies.

You turn away from Jordan and march up the path. You don't want Jordan to see the smile on your face and your reddening cheeks. You like him, but he hasn't earned the right to know that, yet.

After what seems like hours, the river comes into view. It looks clean and its flow is strong. The croaking din grows louder.

"Where is that noise coming from?" Jordan asks.

"It's coming from across the river," you say, craning your head toward the river. "From...that."

You point at a large, green mound on the opposite bank of the river.

"You mean that hill?" Jordan inquires.

"That's not a hill," you reply. "It's frogs. Thousands of frogs, piled on top of each other."

"That doesn't sound good," Jordan says.

"It's not," you reply. "That smell of blood is coming from the river. It must be a dead animal in there. Something big, like a deer."

"Then something in the river killed the big animal and has the frogs spooked," Jordan says.

"Yeah," you reply.

"Well, we can't just stand here," Jordan says. "And it's too far to walk back. We'll be caught out there in the dark and we do *not* want that."

"Yeah, I know," you say. "Let's go check the river out, but be ready."

"Ready for what?"

"Anything," you reply, creeping toward the river. Fear beats in your chest like a djembe drum.

The croaking of the frogs grows louder; more rapid.

You reach the bank of the river. The water is clean and clear. You thrust your index finger into it – the river is oddly warm – as warm as a baby's bath.

"Terry," Jordan whispers, placing a firm hand on your shoulder. "We gotta go."

"What? Why?" You whisper in reply.

"I see lines," Jordan says. "*Hundreds* of them...and they all lead away from here."

"And what does that mean?" You ask.

"It means any place is safer than this one," Jordan answers.

A gurgling noise rises from the river. You look down at the water – scores of bubbles shoot to the surface. A cloud of steam and a wave of heat surge from the river.

"Too late," Jordan sighs, scrambling backward from the steam.

A column of hot water erupts from the river, rising high above the surface of the water. You spy something large, glowing crimson, within the column.

You and Jordan scurry away from the river. The cloud of steam grows into a thick fog that falls all around you like a blanket, stinging your flesh and clouding even your acute vision. You hear a thunderous din and the ground shakes. The hot, moist air threatens to smother you.

After a short while, the fog dissipates. Crouching before you and Jordan is a snarling tiger, which would be frightening enough; however, this tiger is not a creature of flesh and blood, but one of iron and fire.

The metal monster – nearly twice as large as the huge Siberian tiger –smiles sardonically, baring its razor-sharp, iron teeth and the raging fire within its maw. Its eyes, stripes and the end of its tail are red-hot flames. Its claws, more like scimitars, scratch at the earth, rending dirt and stone. It reeks of burnt metal.

"Damn," Jordan says.

"Yeah," you sigh. "This sucks."

"Should we even *try* to run?" Jordan asks.

"Nope," you reply. "It'll probably catch us. It *is* a tiger, after all."

Jordan raises his throwing cudgels above his shoulders. "Well, I guess we fight, then."

"I guess so," you say, raising your macuahuitl. "He's big, he's iron, he's fire, he has teeth and claws like swords..."

"That doesn't sound good for us,"

Jordan chimes in.

"But he's not intelligent," you say. "Not even *animal* intelligent. We'll just outsmart this bucket of bolts."

"Is that so?" The iron tiger roars.

"You were saying?" Jordan sighs.

"I assure you, I have not come to slay you. And that *would* be the end result of a violent encounter with me, by the way."

"What do you want with us, then?" You ask, still holding your weapon at the ready.

"I want you to accompany me to what you call Guatemala City," the creature replies. "There is a pyramid there. Your blood is the key to opening it."

"Our blood?" Jordan says. "How *much* blood?"

"All of it," the iron tiger replies. "But, you are the Keys; your exsanguinations at the foot of the great pyramid are necessary for you to be reborn as the gods you are destined to become. Your Locksmith did not tell you this?"

"Um...no," you reply. "And losing all

of my blood isn't at the top of my lists of things to do."

"Do this and you will be granted power and riches beyond your wildest imaginations."

"That sounds familiar," Jordan says. "So, you serve Henry the Navigator, huh?"

"I am the Gnarl!" The monster roars. "I serve no one!"

The smell of pepper and juniper fills the air.

"That's good," you reply. "Because Henry the Navigator is a powerless, pompous creep with a lame haircut."

"Terry, what the heck are you doing?" Jordan whispers. "I know you smell that juniper. Henry's nearby!"

"Very near," you say, nodding toward the Gnarl.

A sound like distant thunder rumbles within the Gnarl's throat. It roars, opening its toothy maw wide.

You peer into the Gnarl's mouth, past the crimson flames and within you spot...organs. Flesh and blood organs.

Jordan, it's Henry!" You shout.

Jordan hurls the pair of itemo lindaa into the Gnarl's mouth.

"I know," he says. "I saw a path leading into its mouth when it roared."

The Gnarl staggers backward, hissing and coughing. It convulses violently, thrashing about on its belly and sides.

The throwing cudgels, now aflame, fly out of the Gnarl's mouth and speed toward Jordan.

Jordan extends his hands toward the flaming discs.

"Jordan...no!" You scream.

"What?" Jordan inquires.

He can't see the fire! You think.

The discs fly into Jordan's palms. A heartbeat later, his hands burst into flames. Jordan screams shaking his arms furiously. The fire rushes up his arms and then engulfs his face. Jordan's flaming dreadlocks dance upon his shoulders, igniting his shirt. Jordan's entire body is soon blanketed in a raging flame. Jordan screams in agony.

"Jordan!" You cry.

Suddenly, Jordan's screams stop. He stands, calmly, as the fires continue to burn.

"Jordan?" You whisper, slack-jawed.

The bonfire that is your friend turns toward you.

"I'm okay," he says. "I don't know how, but I am."

"Not for long."

You spin around, crouching low, with your macuahuitl held above your head.

"Lower your weapon, child," the Gnarl commands. "Or I will stop holding back the hungry fire that aches to consume your friend."

"Don't do it, Terry," Jordan shouts through the flames. "Henry needs both of us. He won't let me die."

"You're wrong, child. The Gnarl growls. "There is another like you. Only one of you need live. Now, lower that weapon!"

You bring your macuahuitl to your side. "Another?"

"Poor child. There is so much your

Locksmith hasn't told you," the Gnarl
says. "There is a young man in Georgia
from among the Muskogee native people.
He is a shape-shifter and a child of the
Oyo-Aztec Alliance."

"Shapeshifter?" You say.

The Gnarl begins to circle you,
creeping as if he is stalking an animal in
the bush. "Yes. His totem is the bear. At
certain cycles of the moon, he becomes his
totem. I would have approached him long
ago, but he can be quite...disagreeable."

"So, we're easier prey?" You ask,
turning your head toward the Gnarl,
careful to keep the monster in your sight.

"Your powers are more subtle," the
Gnarl replies. "Better suited to stealth
than confrontation."

"If I agree to go with you, will you
free Jordan from those flames?" You ask.

"Of course," the Gnarl replies.
"Jordan is still valuable and I'm sure the
two of us can convince him to join us on
our journey."

The distant thunder in the Gnarl's
chest grows louder; more rapid.

He's lying, you think.

"And do you promise not to stink so badly?" You ask. "The smell of that juniper and pepper is gross!"

The fire that is the Gnarl's eyes changes from red to bright orange. "What?!"

You slash with the macuahuitl, rending the Gnarl's open maw.

The iron tiger howls in agony. Its lower jaw falls to the soft ground with a thud. A stream of lava pours out of the Gnarl's wounded face, scorching the earth.

"Jordan, run to the river!" You shout. "Jump in!"

Jordan takes off, sprinting toward the water.

The flames around him grow higher.

Jordan continues to run toward the river, screaming in agony.

The Gnarl shakes its head, sending lava flying in all directions.

A tiny wad of lava splashes onto your shoulder, searing your clothing and your flesh.

You scream as you fall to the ground on your belly. Desperate, you slash the Gnarl's foreleg. Sparks fly as you rend the metal with your macuahuitl.

The Gnarl collapses onto its side, roaring madly.

"You...are powerful...girl," the Gnarl coughs. "But...not powerful enough...to save your...friend."

You roll to your feet and turn toward the river. Jordan has made it to the bank, but the flames around him have grown into a raging column of fire reaching toward the sky. You can no longer see Jordan through the flames, but you can still hear him scream.

After a few moments, the column of flame around Jordan dissipates, leaving behind a smoking pile of charred bones.

"Jordan!" You scream. "No!"

You snap your head toward the Gnarl, tears staining your face, which is twisted into a mask of pain and rage.

You leap high into the air, raising the macuahuitl above your head.

"No!" The Gnarl roars.

You bring the macuahuitl down upon the Gnarl's neck with all the force you can muster. The weapon severs the monster's head, cutting through iron as if it was paper.

Suddenly, the world seems to shift; to tilt. The Gnarl and the river begin to fade, finally giving way to darkness.

A moment later, you find yourself back in the room with the strange runes beneath the motel.

Sombra stands before you, smiling. "You made it!"

She cranes her neck, peeking around you. "Where's Jordan?"

You feel heat rising up the back of your neck and anger rising with it.

"Gone, thanks to you!" You reply. "You sent us to that crazy place to die!"

"I sent you to become who you were destined to be," Sombra says. "I thought you would be gone much longer; you were gone but a moment – less than four breaths. There is much more for you to do."

"I killed Henry," you say. "He was embodied in an iron monster called the Gnarl. What more *is* there?"

"You killed him in one realm of existence," Sombra replies. "So, another duplicate is dead, but Henry's spirit lives on in *this* world."

"Then, let's find him and end him, once and for all!" You shout.

"I know you want to avenge Jordan's death," Sombra says. "And you'll have your chance, but right now, we must find the next Key. There must be two of you."

"The *next* Key?" You say. "You mean that Native American kid in Georgia? How many of us *are* there?"

"So, Henry told you," Sombra replies. "There aren't many of you…Three; perhaps four. Now, let's go. Time is of the essence."

If you go with Sombra in search of the new Key, go to page 227.

If you refuse to go with Sombra, go to page 229.

"There's a weird croaking noise coming from the right path," Terry says. "But I smell a river. Maybe we can follow it to a place where people are nearby and they can tell us where we are."

"Maybe," you reply. "But what's that croaking?" Frogs?

"If it *is* frogs, there must be thousands of them," Terry says. "They're *loud*. Oh, I also smell blood."

"Animal? Human?" you ask.

"I don't know."

"Well, only one way to find out," you say, tracing a wide arc in the air with your arm and pointing down the footpath. "After you, milady."

Terry holds her weapon chest-high and steps onto the path. You follow a few paces behind her.

You can't help but admire Terry's curvaceous, well-toned form and her feline stride.

"Best view ever!" You say.

Terry peers over her shoulder and rolls her eyes. "Try not to act like a ten year old, okay?"

"There is no try," you reply. "Only do or don't."

"Then, *do*," she says.

"I'll try," you reply.

Terry turns away from you and marches up the path.

You hope you didn't insult her. You want her to like you, but maybe you need to rethink your approach. Terry seems to have more respect for herself than the young women you're used to.

Somehow, that makes her even more *attractive*, you think.

After what seems like hours, the river comes into view. A loud, croaking din greets you.

"Where is that noise coming from?" you ask.

"It's coming from across the river," Terry says, craning her head toward the river. "From…that."

She points at a large, green mound on the opposite bank of the river.

"You mean that hill?" you say.

"That's not a hill," Terry replies. "It's

frogs. Thousands of frogs piled on top of each other."

"That doesn't sound good," you sigh.

"It's not," Terry replies. "That smell of blood is coming from the river. It must be a dead animal in there. Something big, like a deer."

"Then something in the river killed the big animal and has the frogs spooked," you say.

"Yeah," Terry replies.

"Well, we can't just stand here," you say. "And it's too far to walk back. We'll be caught out there in the dark and we do *not* want that."

"Yeah, I know," Terry says. "Let's go check the river out, but be ready."

"Ready for what?"

"Anything," she replies, creeping toward the river.

The croaking of the frogs grows louder; more rapid.

You reach the bank of the river. The water is clean and clear. Terry thrusts her index finger into it. "It's warm," she says.

Suddenly, crimson lines – hundreds of them – appear before you. The glowing lines all lead away from the riverbank. Fear pounds in your chest like a djembe drum.

"Terry," you whisper, placing a firm hand on her shoulder. "We gotta go."

"What? Why?" She whispers in reply.

"I see lines," you say. "*Hundreds* of them...and they all lead away from here."

"And what does that mean?" Terry asks.

"It means any place is safer than this one," you answer.

A gurgling noise rises from the river. You look down at the water – scores of bubbles shoot to the surface. A cloud of steam and a wave of heat surge from the river.

"Too late," you sigh, scrambling backward from the steam.

A column of hot water erupts from the river, rising high above the surface of the water. You spy something large, glowing crimson, within the column.

You and Terry scurry away from the river. The cloud of steam grows into a thick fog that falls all around you like a blanket, stinging your flesh and clouding even your acute vision. You hear a thunderous din and the ground shakes. The hot, moist air threatens to smother you.

After a short while, the fog dissipates. Crouching before you and Terry is a snarling tiger, which would be frightening enough; however, this tiger is not a creature of flesh and blood, but one of iron and fire.

The metal monster – nearly twice as large as the huge Siberian tiger –smiles sardonically, baring its razor-sharp, iron teeth and the raging fire within its maw. Its eyes, stripes and the end of its tail are red-hot flames. Its claws, more like scimitars, scratch at the earth, rending dirt and stone. It reeks of burnt metal.

"Damn," you gasp.

"Yeah," Terry sighs. "This sucks."

"Should we even *try* to run?" You ask.

"Nope," Terry replies. "It'll probably catch us. It *is* a tiger, after all."

You raise your throwing cudgels above your shoulders. "Well, I guess we fight, then."

"I guess so," Terry says, raising her macuahuitl. "He's big, he's iron, he's fire, he has teeth and claws like swords..."

"That doesn't sound good for us," you chime in.

"But he's not intelligent," she says. "Not even *animal* intelligent. We'll just outsmart this bucket of bolts."

"Is that so?" The iron tiger roars.

You glare at Terry. "You were saying?"

"I assure you, I have not come to slay you. And that *would* be the end result of a violent encounter with me, by the way."

"What do you want with us, then?" Terry asks, still holding her weapon at the ready.

"I want you to accompany me to what you call Guatemala City," the creature replies. "There is a pyramid there. Your blood is the key to opening it."

"Our blood?" you say. "How *much*

blood?"

"All of it," the iron tiger replies. "But, you are the Keys; your exsanguinations at the foot of the great pyramid are necessary for you to be reborn as the gods you are destined to become. Your Locksmith did not tell you this?"

"Um...no," Terry replies. "And losing all of my blood isn't at the top of my lists of things to do."

"Do this and you will be granted power and riches beyond your wildest imaginations."

"That sounds familiar," you say, remembering Henry's words back at the Pyramid Arena. "So, you serve Henry the Navigator, huh?"

"I am the Gnarl!" The monster roars. "I serve no one!"

The smell of pepper and juniper fills the air.

"That's good," Terry replies. "Because Henry the Navigator is a powerless, pompous creep with a lame haircut."

"Terry, what the heck are you doing?" you whisper. "I know you smell that juniper. Henry's nearby!"

"Very near," Terry says, nodding toward the Gnarl.

The Gnarl roars, opening its toothy maw wide.

Terry peers into the Gnarl's mouth. Her eyes grow wide as she sees something inside the creature that shocks her.

A crimson line appears, stretching from your throwing cudgels to the inside of the Gnarl's mouth.

Jordan, it's Henry!" Terry shouts.

You hurl the pair of itemo lindaa into the Gnarl's mouth.

"I know," you say. "I saw a path leading into its mouth when it roared."

The Gnarl staggers backward, hissing and coughing. It convulses violently, thrashing about on its belly and sides.

The throwing cudgels fly out of the Gnarl's mouth and speed toward you.

You extend your hands toward the speeding discs.

"Jordan...no!" Terry screams.

"What?" You inquire.

Terry looks frightened, you think. *Why? I've caught the discs several times now. They hit hard, but, for some reason, they do not hurt my hands when I catch them.*

The discs fly into your palms.

No pain, as always, you think. *Why does Terry look so concerned?*

A heartbeat later, your hands burst into flames.

What the...? You think. *My itemo lindaa...Terry must have seen them aflame. But why couldn't I? This...hurts!*

You scream shaking your arms furiously. The fire rushes up your arms and then engulfs your face. Your flesh feels as if you are being stuck with a thousand needles. Your dreadlocks, now ablaze, dance upon your shoulders, igniting your shirt. Soon, your entire body is blanketed in a raging flame. You scream in agony.

"Jordan!" Terry cries.

Suddenly, the pain stops. The fires continue to burn, but you feel no more pain.

"Jordan?" Terry whispers, slack-jawed.

You turn toward Terry. "I'm okay. I don't know how, but I am."

"Not for long."

Terry spins around, crouching low, with her macuahuitl held above her head.

"Lower your weapon, child," the Gnarl commands. "Or I will stop holding back the hungry fire that aches to consume your friend."

"Don't do it, Terry," you shout through the flames. "Henry needs both of us. He won't let me die."

"You're wrong, child. The Gnarl growls. "There is another like you. Only one of you need live. Now, lower that weapon!"

Terry brings her macuahuitl to her side. "Another?"

"Poor child. There is so much your Locksmith hasn't told you," the Gnarl says. "There is a young man in Georgia from among the Muskogee native people. He is a shape-shifter and a child of the Oyo-Aztec Alliance."

"Shapeshifter?" Terry says.

Like a werewolf? You think.

The Gnarl begins to circle Terry, creeping as if he is stalking an animal in the bush. "Yes. His totem is the bear. At certain cycles of the moon, he becomes his totem. I would have approached him long ago, but he can be quite...disagreeable."

"So, we're easier prey?" Terry asks, turning her head toward the Gnarl, careful to keep the monster in her sight.

"Your powers are more subtle," the Gnarl replies. "Better suited to stealth than confrontation."

"If I agree to go with you, will you free Jordan from those flames?" Terry asks.

"Of course," the Gnarl replies. "Jordan is still valuable and I'm sure the two of us can convince him to join us on our journey."

"And do you promise not to stink so badly?" Terry asks. "The smell of that juniper and pepper is gross!"

The fire that is the Gnarl's eyes changes from red to bright orange. "What?!"

Terry slashes with the macuahuitl, rending the Gnarl's open maw.

The iron tiger howls in agony. Its lower jaw falls to the soft ground with a thud. A stream of lava pours out of the Gnarl's wounded face, scorching the earth.

"Jordan, run to the river!" Terry shouts. "Jump in!"

Terry must have realized the Gnarl is lying.

You take off, sprinting toward the water.

The flames around you grow higher.

Oh no.

You continue to run toward the river, but the pain returns.

You scream as the flames char your flesh.

The Gnarl's agonized roar fades as your inner ear is burned away. You try to look toward Terry, but you can only see darkness because your eyes have melted. You know that soon, the fire will have totally consumed you, but you hope that Terry destroys the Gnarl and makes it out of this strange place okay.

You are in so much despair.

So much pain.

So much...

The End

"The center path scares me," you say, sniffing the air.

"Why?" Jordan asks. "What's wrong?"

"I smell roses and freshly cut grass," you reply. "I hear birds chirping and the faint sound of something, panting, like a dog after a romp in the garden."

Jordan's brow furrows. "Yeah, that sounds about as scary as a Chihuahua puppy sleeping on a fluffy pillow."

"That's just it," you say. "It's *too* peaceful. We know why we're here – Sombra wants to force the powers within us to surface through conflict and adversity."

"So, the peaceful environment you sense is just a cover over something worse," Jordan sighs.

"Or a trap," you reply.

"Only one way to find out for sure," Jordan says, shooting a glance at the center path.

"Yep," you reply with a shrug. "Let's do it! Mi madre always says if something scares you, run to it."

"*My* mama always says if something scares you...just run." Jordan says. "But hey, let's do like white folks in a scary movie and investigate."

You laugh. You're starting to really like Jordan. You know he will become a great friend – one of your best – and, with a little more maturity, maybe something more. You'd never tell him that, of course.

You walk down the path with Jordan close behind you. After several minutes, the path ends, disappearing under well-manicured grass, scattered rose bushes and dry oak leaves colored bright green, orange and red.

In the distance, across the expanse of grass, trees and rose bushes, stands a stately manor house.

"See the safest way into that house, Jordan?" You ask.

"I see a line that curves around the right side of it," Jordan replies. "We should..."

Jordan's brow furrows. He raises his throwing cudgels to the height of his shoulders.

"What is it?" You ask, raising your macuahuitl and crouching low. "What do you see, now?"

"Several zigzagging, broken lines," Jordan says. "All leading to that house."

"What does that mean?"

"It means something in that house is about to hit us hard and fast," Jordan says. "Whenever my team would ball against another team that was about to do a fast break, I'd see these same lines."

"Okay, break that down in non-basketball-fan terms," you reply.

"A fast break is an offensive strategy," Jordan says. "A team tries to move the ball up court and into scoring position as quickly as possible, so the defense is outnumbered, off-balance and doesn't have time to set up their own attack."

"But I don't see, smell, or hear anything," you say, "But the trees, grass and roses."

"I think we're about to find out," Jordan says, pointing toward the house.

You snap your head toward the mansion. The mahogany door is now open wide. An overpowering gamy odor assaults you, making you want to gag. A moment later, a horde of large, dark brown mandrills pours out of the house, snarling, as they leap and scurry off of the porch and onto the walkway and grass.

"O...M...G!" Jordan gasps.

A huge mandrill, standing upright lumbers out of the house and stands at the edge of the top step. This mandrill, twice the size of its brethren, wears a spiked, crimson leather vest and matching bracers over its alabaster fur.

The big mandrill saunters down the stairs and stands on the walkway with its sinewy arms crossed over its barrel chest. The horde of snarling mandrills gather around their leader and then fix their hungry gaze on you.

"Ever fought a baboon before?" You whisper.

"Mandrill!" The large, albino mandrill bellows. "Mandrill stronger than baboon...Mandrill smarter than baboon...baboon of one color; mandrill of many. Mandrill most beautiful creature in world. Baboon not!"

"Please, forgive my ignorance," you say. "My friend and I did not mean to trespass upon your home."

"And a lovely home it is, too," Jordan says. "We'll leave you to it."

"Boy and girl can't leave," the alabaster mandrill says. "Boy and girl key. Father need key to open lock."

"Father?" You say. "Who is your father?"

"Not blood father," the big mandrill answers. "Blood father is Neeb, King of Mandrill. I am Abogo, General of Mandrill army. No-blood father is Henry the Navigator, who make Abogo smartest

Mandrill of all time."

"Henry is an evil man, Abogo," you say. "He's using you to do bad things."

"Yeah," Jordan says. "Do a *good* thing and let us go."

Abogo smiles, revealing a mouth full of wicked teeth. "Father say you say that. Father also say we can't kill you, but we *can* hurt you bad if you not come with Abogo. He promise to fix you, though."

"We don't want to fight you, Abogo," Jordan says.

"Abogo know you don't" Abogo replies. "You can't beat Mandrill. Who want fight what can't beat?"

"Who want *beat* what can't *fight*?" Jordan says, smiling weakly.

"Abogo do," Abogo says. "It easy win."

You peer over at Jordan, awaiting his comeback. Jordan shrugs.

"I got nothin'," he says.

"Enough jibba-jabba," Abogo roars. "Come, now...or fight!"

A *whoosh* of wind passes your ear. A moment later, one of Jordan's itemo lindaa slams into Abogo's brow.

The albino mandrill staggers backward, roaring madly.

"Fight, it is, then," you say with a shrug. You charge toward the snarling mandrills with your macuahuitl at the ready.

The throwing cudgel ricochets off of Abogo's skull. Jordan leaps high into the air and catches it.

The mandrills bolt toward you.

Jordan hurls both cudgels into the crowd of mandrills just before he lands from his leap.

One itemo lindaa strikes a mandrill in his chest. A weak croak escapes the creature's lips as it tumbles backward, landing, face down, in a thorny rose bush.

The other cudgel crashes into a

mandrill's knee. A loud *crack* follows the blow. The mandrill's knee collapses backward. The wailing creature falls to the ground, its red eyes maddened by agony.

A mandrill slashes at your face with the razor sharp claws of its right paw.

You twist your shoulders to the right.

The mandrill's strike whizzes by, just missing you.

You slash downward with your macuahuitl, cutting a deep gash in the mandrill's forearm.

The mandrill's arm flops lifelessly at its side. The creature whirls toward you, slashing at you with its left arm.

You duck the blow and then slash upward into the creature's armpit.

The mandrill's left arm falls to its side, as lifeless as the right one.

You spin backward on your right heel as you whip your left leg in a wide arc behind you. The heel of your left foot slams into the side of the mandrill's face. Its lower jaw jerks out of the socket. The mandrill's eyes roll back toward its brow just before the creature slumps onto its back.

Something slams into your gut, forcing the air from your lungs. You fly backward, screaming silence. You focus through your pain. Abogo stands before you, smiling broadly, growing smaller as you careen across the garden. You feel the macuahuitl pulse in your fist. You thrust the weapon into the earth, halting your flight. You take a knee, holding onto the macuahuitl with both hands for support.

Abogo pounds his chest and roars. The mandrills skitter sideways, leaving a wide path for their captain. The giant white mandrill gallops toward you, rending the earth and sending grass and dirt flying with each step.

You sip the air, struggling desperately to bring oxygen back to your lungs.

Abogo closes on you, raising his massive arms above his head, in preparation for a crippling blow with his claws.

"Terry, brace yourself!" You hear Jordan shout.

A moment later, you feel something heavy on your shoulders. You look toward your right and see Jordan's sneaker near your face.

Jordan leaps off your shoulders, his arms crossed at his chest. He snaps his hands toward the earth, releasing the pair of itemo lindaa.

The cudgels slice into Abogo's feet, rending flesh, tendon and bone. His severed toes bounce across the grass.

Abogo's eyes grow wide as saucers. He lets loose a high pitched cry as he stumbles forward.

The air returns to your lungs.

Abogo falls, his gargantuan body collapsing toward you.

You spring to your feet, slashing upward in a figure-eight motion.

Abogo crashes to the ground. His head rolls past you, resting at the feet of a horrified mandrill.

The horde of mandrills raise their faces toward the sky and, in unison, howl in sorrow for their fallen leader and beloved brother.

Jordan presses his back against yours. "Come on," he shouts. "Come suffer the same fate as your captain!"

The mandrills turn their gaze toward you. They roar as one.

You crouch low, preparing to fight beside Jordan to your final breath.

Surprisingly, the mandrills creep backward, still roaring as they disappear into the shadow of the trees.

"Whew," Jordan gasps. "That was close."

"I know, right," you reply. "Strangely, I wasn't afraid to fight...or to die."

"Same here," Jordan says. "Maybe

there's something to this *Keys* thing."

"No doubt," you say. "I guess we'll find out how right Sombra is when we take this fight to Henry."

"We're going in the house, then?" Jordan says.

"Yeah," you reply. "It's time to finish this."

"Let's do it," he says.

You sprint toward the mansion. Jordan runs beside you. You bound up the steps toward the door. You dash inside the house...

A moment later, you find yourself back in the room with the strange runes beneath the motel.

Sombra stands before you, smiling. "You made it!"

You feel heat rising up the back of your neck and anger rising with it.

"No thanks to you!" You reply. "You sent us to that crazy place to die!"

"I sent you to become who you were destined to be," Sombra says. "I thought you would be gone much longer; you were gone but a moment – less than four breaths. There is much more for you to do."

"We killed Henry's mandrill general, Abogo," you say. "We would have killed Henry too. What happened?"

"You fulfilled what you needed to fulfill," Sombra replies. "Killing Henry is not necessary – at this time – to awaken the Gods in you."

"So, we're ready now?" Jordan asks.

"Not quite," Sombra answers. "The Gods within you are now awakened, but they are like a man shocked out of sleep by an alarm clock – groggy; disoriented; in need of a few moments to become fully aware and focused."

"Then, let's wake them up and be done with this," Jordan says. "I'm ready to deal with Henry, get those pyramids going once and for all and go home!"

"Same here!" You reply.

"That is the Gods within you talking," Sombra says. "They are eager to meet their destiny; *your* destiny. And they…*you* will have your chance, but right now, we must rendezvous with the third

Key. I sense that we will need him in the final battle with Henry the Navigator and his dark army."

"The *third* Key?" You say. "How many of us *are* there?"

"Just the three of you, we believe; perhaps four," Sombra replies.

"Maybe *four*?" Jordan says.

"All will be revealed in due time," Sombra replies. "Now, let's go. Time is of the essence."

If you go with Sombra in search of the new Key, go to page 227.

If you refuse to go with Sombra, go to page 229.

"The center path scares me," Terry says, sniffing the air.

"Why?" you ask. "What's wrong?"

"I smell roses and freshly cut grass," Terry replies. "I hear birds chirping and the faint sound of something, panting, like a dog after a romp in the garden."

Your brow furrows. "Yeah, that sounds about as scary as a Chihuahua puppy sleeping on a fluffy pillow."

"That's just it," Terry says. "It's *too* peaceful. We know why we're here – Sombra wants to force the powers within us to surface through conflict and adversity."

"So, the peaceful environment you sense is just a cover over something worse," You sigh.

"Or a trap," Terry replies.

"Only one way to find out for sure," you say, shooting a glance at the center path.

"Yep," Terry replies with a shrug. "Let's do it! Mi madre always says if something scares you, run to it."

"*My* mama always says if something scares you...just run." You say. "But hey, let's do like white folks in a scary movie and investigate."

Terry laughs.

I think Terry is starting to like me, you think. You know Terry will become a great friend – one of your best – and, if she softens up a bit and if you can stay focused and talk about something more than basketball or how good she looks, maybe the two of you can be something more. *Only time will tell.*

You walk down the path with Terry – and her animal-like senses – leading the way. After several minutes, the path ends, disappearing under well-manicured grass, scattered rose bushes and dry oak leaves colored bright green, orange and red.

In the distance, across the expanse of grass, trees and rose bushes, stands a stately manor house.

"See the safest way into that house, Jordan?" Terry asks.

"I see a line that curves around the right side of it," you reply. "We should…"

Suddenly a pattern appears on the ground before you; a pattern that sends a chill racing up your spine.

"What is it?" Terry asks, raising her macuahuitl and crouching low. "What do you see, now?"

"Several zigzagging, broken lines," you say. "All leading to that house."

"What does that mean?"

"It means something in that house is about to hit us hard and fast," You say. "Whenever my team would ball against another team that was about to do a fast break, I'd see these same lines."

"Okay, break that down in non-basketball-fan terms," Terry replies.

"A fast break is an offensive strategy," you say. "A team tries to move the ball up court and into scoring position as quickly as possible, so the defense is outnumbered, off-balance and doesn't have time to set up their own attack."

"But I don't see, smell, or hear anything," Terry says, "Except the trees, grass and roses."

"I think we're about to find out," You say, pointing toward the house.

You snap your head toward the mansion. The mahogany door is now open wide. A faint, gamy odor emanates from inside the house. A moment later, a horde of large, dark brown mandrills pours out of the house, snarling, as they leap and scurry off of the porch and onto the walkway and grass.

"O...M...G!" You gasp.

A huge mandrill, standing upright lumbers out of the house and stands at the edge of the top step. This mandrill, twice the size of its brethren, wears a spiked, crimson leather vest and matching bracers over its alabaster fur.

The big mandrill saunters down the stairs and stands on the walkway with its sinewy arms crossed over its barrel chest. The horde of snarling mandrills gather around their leader and then fix their hungry gaze on you.

"Ever fought a baboon before?" You whisper.

"Mandrill!" The large, albino mandrill bellows. "Mandrill stronger than baboon…Mandrill smarter than baboon…baboon of one color; Mandrill of many. Mandrill most beautiful creature in world. Baboon not!"

"Please, forgive my ignorance," Terry says. "My friend and I did not mean to trespass upon your home."

"And a lovely home it is, too," you say. "We'll leave you to it."

"Boy and girl can't leave," the alabaster mandrill says. "Boy and girl key. Father need key to open lock."

"Father?" You say. "Who is your father?"

"Not blood father," the big mandrill answers. "Blood father is Neeb, King of

Mandrill. I am Abogo, General of Mandrill army. No-blood father is Henry the Navigator, who make Abogo smartest Mandrill of all time."

"Henry is an evil man, Abogo," Terry says. "He's using you to do bad things."

"Yeah," you say. "Do a *good* thing and let us go."

Abogo smiles, revealing a mouth full of wicked teeth. "Father say you say that. Father also say we can't kill you, but we *can* hurt you bad if you not come with Abogo. He promise to fix you, though."

"We don't want to fight you, Abogo," you say.

"Abogo know you don't" Abogo replies. "You can't beat Mandrill. Who want fight what can't beat?"

"Who want *beat* what can't *fight*?" You say, smiling weakly.

"Abogo do," Abogo says. "It easy win."

Terry peers at you, awaiting your

comeback. You shrug.

"I got nothin'," you say with a smirk.

"Enough jibba-jabba," Abogo roars. "Come, now…or fight!"

The itemo lindaa grow hot in your hands, signaling their need to be released. You let the one in your right hand fly with a downward snap of your arm. The throwing cudgel whizzes past Terry and then slams into Abogo's brow.

The albino mandrill staggers backward, roaring madly.

"Fight, it is, then," Terry says with a shrug. She charges toward the snarling mandrills with her macuahuitl at the ready.

The throwing cudgel ricochets off of Abogo's skull. You leap high into the air and catch it.

The mandrills bolt toward Terry.

You hurl both cudgels into the crowd of mandrills just before you land from your leap.

One itemo lindaa strikes a mandrill in his chest. A weak croak escapes the creature's lips as it tumbles backward, landing, face down, in a thorny rose bush.

The other cudgel crashes into a mandrill's knee. A loud *crack* follows the blow. The mandrill's knee collapses backward. The wailing creature falls to the ground, its red eyes maddened by agony.

A mandrill slashes at Terry's face with the razor sharp claws of its right paw.

She twists her shoulders to the right.

The mandrill's strike whizzes by, just missing her.

Terry slashes downward with your macuahuitl, cutting a deep gash in the mandrill's forearm.

The mandrill's arm flops lifelessly at its side. The creature whirls toward her, slashing at her with its left arm.

Terry ducks the blow and then slashes upward into the creature's armpit.

The mandrill's left arm falls to its side, as lifeless as the right one.

A mandrill dives toward you with its toothy maw open wide. You leap into the air, your leg disappearing out of reach just before the creature's wicked fangs close around it. You hurl both itemo lindaa. One cudgel crashes into the top of the mandrill's skull; the other, into the base of its neck.

The creature convulses violently and then collapses, in a heap, onto its side.

You turn your focus toward Terry just in time to see Abogo's fist slam into her gut like a wrecking ball. Terry flies backward. Her mouth is open wide as if she is screaming but no sound comes from it. Terry seems to fight against the pain and against her deflated lungs. She thrusts her macuahuitl into the earth, halting her flight. She takes a knee, holding onto the macuahuitl with both of her hands for support.

Abogo pounds his chest and roars. The mandrills skitter sideways, leaving a wide path for their captain. The giant white mandrill gallops toward Terry, rending the earth and sending grass and dirt flying with each step.

Abogo closes on Terry, raising his massive arms above his head, in preparation for a crippling blow with his claws.

"Terry, brace yourself!" You shout as you explode forward, sprinting toward your kneeling friend.

You leap, landing on Terry's shoulders and then, using her shoulders as a spring, leap again, toward the giant mandrill.

You cross your arms at your chest then snap your hands toward the earth, releasing the pair of itemo lindaa.

The cudgels slice into Abogo's feet, rending flesh, tendon and bone. His severed toes bounce across the grass.

Abogo's eyes grow wide as saucers. He lets loose a high pitched cry as he stumbles under you and toward Terry.

You catch the itemo lindaa and then

land in a crouched position.

Abogo falls forward, his gargantuan body collapsing toward Terry.

Terry springs to her feet, slashing upward in a figure-eight motion.

Abogo crashes to the ground. His head rolls past Terry, resting at the feet of a horrified mandrill.

The horde of mandrills raise their faces toward the sky and, in unison, howl in sorrow for their fallen leader and beloved brother.

You press your back against Terry's. "Come on," you shout at the mandrills. "Come suffer the same fate as your captain!"

The mandrills turn their gaze toward you. They roar as one.

You crouch low, preparing to fight beside Terry to your final breath.

Surprisingly, the mandrills creep backward, still roaring as they disappear into the shadow of the trees.

"Whew," you gasp. "That was close."

"I know, right," Terry replies. "Strangely, I wasn't afraid to fight...or to die."

"Same here," you say. "Maybe there's something to this *Keys* thing."

"No doubt," Terry says. "I guess we'll find out how right Sombra is when we take this fight to Henry."

"We're going in the house, then?" You say.

"Yeah," Terry replies. "It's time to finish this."

"Let's do it," you say.

You sprint toward the mansion. Terry runs beside you. You bound up the steps toward the door. You dash inside the house...

A moment later, you find yourself back in the room with the strange runes beneath the motel.

Sombra stands before you, smiling. "You made it!"

You feel heat rising up the back of your neck and anger rising with it.

"No thanks to you!" You reply. "You sent us to that crazy place to die!"

"I sent you to become who you were destined to be," Sombra says. "I thought you would be gone much longer; you were gone but a moment – less than four breaths. There is much more for you to do."

"We killed Henry's mandrill general, Abogo," you say. "We would have killed Henry too. What happened?"

"You fulfilled what you needed to fulfill," Sombra replies. "Killing Henry is not necessary – at this time – to awaken the Gods in you."

"So, we're ready now?" Terry asks.

"Not quite," Sombra answers. "The Gods within you are now awakened, but they are like a man shocked out of sleep by an alarm clock – groggy; disoriented; in need of a few moments to become fully aware and focused."

"Then, let's wake them up and be done with this," you say. "I'm ready to deal with Henry, get those pyramids going once and for all and go home!"

"Same here!" Terry replies.

"That is the Gods within you talking," Sombra says. "They are eager to meet their destiny; *your* destiny. And they...*you* will have your chance, but right now, we must rendezvous with the third Key. I sense that we will need him in the final battle with Henry the Navigator and his dark army."

"The *third* Key?" You say. "How many of us *are* there?"

"Just the three of you, we believe; perhaps four," Sombra replies.

"Maybe four?" You say.

"All will be revealed in due time," Sombra replies. "Now, let's go. Time is of the essence."

If you go with Sombra in search of the new Key, go to page 227.

If you refuse to go with Sombra, go to page 229.

You nod. "Let's go."

You follow Sombra up the stairs, out of the temple and then through the office. You trot, side-by-side, to Sombra's station wagon. You hop in and Sombra speeds off.

"Next stop…Georgia," Sombra says. "The Etowah Indian Mounds."

"Pyramids," you whisper.

"Yes," Sombra replies. "And the village of shape-shifters who live beneath them."

"Shape-shifters? Village? *Beneath* them?" You gasp.

"Nothing should surprise you by now," Sombra says. "You still have much to learn."

You agree with Sombra – you *do* have much to learn; much more. You hope you learn fast. You've witnessed how powerful Henry the Navigator is and you know that you're going to need to know a lot more if you hope to survive, let alone prevail.

The End

*For the continuing adventures of Terry De Fuego and Jordan Drummond, their battle against Henry the Navigator and his terrifying army and their quest to awaken the Gods within and the Pyramids around the world, look for **The Keys II: Awakening**, coming in 2015!*

"No can, do," you say. "We can do this on our own. There is no need for another Key."

"*We* cannot do anything," Sombra replies. "After I have joined you with the third Key and gotten you safely to the first pyramid, my job is complete. Awakening the pyramids and destroying Henry once and for all will be solely up to the Keys."

"That's awful convenient," you say.

Sombra saunters toward you. You feel a familiar heat and pulsing in your hands.

"Are you calling me a coward?" Sombra inquires, moving closer to you.

"*Are* you one?" You say, taking a small step toward Sombra.

A broad smile spreads across Sombra's face. "Good! You are almost ready." She extends her hand to you. You shake it firmly. "But we need that third Key."

"I told you, I'm not..."

The world begins to tilt. Your vision blurs. "You got me again."

"Yes," Sombra says.

You feel numbness creeping up your legs.

"How?" You ask.

"I soaked my hands in it," Sombra replies. "You'll sleep for a few hours. When you awaken, we'll be at the Etowah Mounds."

"Sombra...you..."

You try to swear at her, but the words are trapped in your throat. The world goes dark. The last thing you remember is the sound of your body hitting the floor and the feeling of sand on your face.

The End

For the continuing adventures of Terry De Fuego and Jordan Drummond, their battle against Henry the Navigator and his *terrifying army and their quest to awaken the Gods within and the Pyramids around the world, look for **The Keys II: Awakening**, coming in 2015!*

YOU are the Hero!

In 1978, an unproven assistant editor in her early twenties, Joëlle Delbourgo got an unwelcome message: her boss at Bantam wanted to see her.

Delbourgo was championing a new children's title called *The Cave of Time*. The book was something of an anomaly – it didn't have a plot or a main character or even a proper ending. Instead, the reader was asked to assume the role of the hero. And *The Cave of Time* wasn't the only book of its kind – it was one book in a series!

The main premise of the books was simple: they weren't meant to be read straight through; instead, each book consisted of a collection of episodes which were read in a certain order depending on the choices the reader made. The reader, as the hero, found himself or herself in a situation faced with a choice of actions; having decided what action to take, he or she proceeded to the page of the book where the consequences of that decision were played out and a new decision then had to be made. Depending on the reader's decisions, the protagonist succeeded or failed; lived or died.

Delbourgo hoped to make it her first major acquisition.

The main premise of the books was simple: they weren't meant to be read straight through; instead, each book consisted of a collection of episodes which were read in a certain order depending on the choices the reader made. The reader, as protagonist, finds himself or herself in a situation and is faced with a choice of actions; having decided what action to take, he or she proceeds to the page of the book where the consequences of that decision are played out and a new decision must be made. Though the reader usually must decide between only two actions, sometimes three or more actions present themselves, with the maximum being five or six. Depending on the reader's decisions, the protagonist succeeds or fails, lives or dies.

In fact, she hoped to pursue the entire series. However, as a junior voice in the company, she had no idea how her higher-ups would respond to such an experimental project. As she stepped into the office of Oscar Dystel, Bantam's president, anxiety struck.

"I understand you're trying to change the way kids read," he barked.

She was. And she wasn't alone.

A decade earlier, an attorney named Edward Packard hit upon an idea that grew from his nights reading bedtime stories to his children. Whenever Packard couldn't figure out how to resolve a story, he asked his children to give him options on how the story should end. He soon realized that they enjoyed the stories more when they helped choose the endings.

This interactivity was a valuable storytelling device – it held the children's attention *and* sparked their innate creativity.

Packard figured if his children enjoyed this form of storytelling, other children would too and he began to contemplate a way to package it in book form. During his commute to and from work, he began to write a shipwreck adventure called *Sugarcane Island*, which had multiple storylines that required reader participation.

In 1969, he passed his finished copy of *Sugarcane Island* along to a friend of a friend who worked as a William Morris literary agent. The feedback was glowing.

"The agent said he would be surprised if there were no takers," Packard recalls. *"Then he proceeded to be surprised."*

Sugarcane Island collected dust until 1975, when Vermont Crossroads Press, a publisher looking for innovative children's books, picked it up. The press was headed by R.A. Montgomery, a former high school teacher who saw the educational value in game structure. According to Montgomery, *"Experiential learning is the most powerful way for kids, or for anyone, to learn something,"*

Montgomery published *Sugarcane Island* to a meager response, but he wasn't discouraged by the small numbers. He and Packard began to write more stories. However, Montgomery's Vermont Crossroads Press didn't have great distribution capability, so he passed the title to a young literary agent named Amy Berkower, who tried to pitch the books to numerous houses.

The only person responsive was Joëlle Delbourgo.

"I got really excited," says Delbourgo, who also worked in Bantam's educational division. *"I said, 'Amy, this is revolutionary.' This is precomputer, remember. The idea of interactive fiction, choosing an ending, was fresh and novel. It tapped into something very fundamental."*

But before Delbourgo could publish the book, she had to persuade her boss at Bantam to take a risk...and corporations are not in the risk-taking business.

Dystel was skeptical at first, but Delbourgo's presentation was convincing. She believed in the product. Dystel wound up becoming Delbourgo's biggest supporter and the *Choose Your Own Adventure* series officially launched in 1979.

Montgomery and Packard were each contracted to write six books. The first title to be picked up by Bantam was Montgomery's *Journey Under the Sea*, about an expedition to Atlantis. Readers were confronted with seismic choices: *If you put up the energy repulsion shields to try and escape the black hole, turn to page 22!*

To stoke attention, Bantam gave away thousands of copies, flooded book fairs, and created teaching guides for classrooms. The strategy worked. By 1981, Bantam had four million copies in print.

That same year, the young daughter of New York Times culture columnist Aljean Harmetz picked up a CYOA book and couldn't put it down. Intrigued, Harmetz wrote a piece that described the series as being "as contagious as chicken pox." That's when the popularity of the books exploded.

To capitalize on the momentum, Bantam decided to roll out one title a month. In turning up the frequency to serial levels, the publisher hit upon another novelty that would prove irresistible. Because the books were numbered sequentially, kids started collecting them like trading cards. Years later, this savvy marketing technique would be applied to other series, including *The Baby-Sitters Club* and my son's favorite series: *Diary of a Wimpy Kid*.

Packard quit his law practice to write full time.

By the late 1980s, the series was showing signs of exhaustion. Crappy concepts like *You Are a Shark* signaled the end was near. Then came the rise of video and computer games, which provided that same interactivity in an even more addictive format so, in 1999 the publisher of the 250 million copy selling powerhouse, *Choose Your Own Adventure* chose to retire the brand and let the trademark lapse.

However, CYOA had – and continues to have – a powerful influence worldwide, inspiring such mega-popular books as *Goosebumps*, and proving to skeptical parents that children were still willing to open a book and read.

I believe the solution to getting reluctant readers to read lies in the CYOA, or gamebook, format.

Back in the late 70s through the late 90s, children around the world – particularly boys, who are often reluctant readers – and *Black* boys, long considered the most reluctant readers – were reading, collecting, trading and discussing the *Choose Your Own Adventure* books.

Why?

Because children were put in the driver's seat. *They* were the mountain climber; *they* were the abominable snowman hunter; *they* were the time traveler and deep-sea explorer. They made the choices, so they read.

This was especially important for Black children who never saw themselves as the hero in books. But in the CYOA books, invariably written in the 2nd Person, the reader becomes "you." YOU fight the bandits; YOU travel by hot air balloon across the Sahara Desert to rescue your friends. Finally, we Black boys could be the hero...even though the illustrations always showed the hero as some white boy. But we'd just ignore the artwork and enjoy being the hero for once. Sad, but true.

Choose Your Own Adventure has been cited by numerous educators as a uniquely effective method for helping students learn to read. The series has documented popular appeal for the reluctant reader due to its interactivity. *Choose Your Own Adventure* has also been used specifically in technology lesson plans in elementary, high school and college curricula, as well as in professional development tools.

The choose-your-own-adventure books are essentially games played by one, and it is not surprising that a related type of book – the role-playing book – has developed. These books are essentially games of chance, with the reader, as hero, deciding the outcome of various decisions by a role of dice and sometimes keeping a score.

The role-playing game-style CYOA books, which use stats and sometimes even dice, similar to *Dungeons and Dragons*, seem to be aimed at high school-aged readers and older, most *Choose Your Own Adventure*-type books seem to be aimed at children between the ages of 10 and 13, though there has been a series for adults and there is presently a series for preschoolers.

In my *YOU are the Hero* series of books, beginning with the Young Adult novel (for ages 12 and older), The Keys, the reader can choose to be either Teresa "Terry" De Fuego, a nineteen year old self-proclaimed extreme journalist of Aztec descent, or Jordan Drummond, nineteen year old math genius and star basketball player of Igbo and Ateke descent.

Whichever of these two strong, independent and cool characters the reader chooses to be, they are encouraged throughout the book to be self-confident enough to forge ahead and complete the adventure, while applying common sense, prudence, and certain moral values in the decision-making process.

Courage is of great importance in *The Keys* and in all of the *YOU are the Hero* books, for unless the hero forges ahead, there is no story.

Reading *The Keys* also helps to instill confidence in young readers and teaches them to trust themselves to do the right thing.

However, courage and confidence should not rule out caution. The successful hero is prudent – thinking before acting and being patient enough to learn all that may be useful later, asking for expert help when he or she needs it, using common sense, and taking the advice of our elders, who are wiser than us.

So, finally, our youth – and we adults, too – can be the hero in Science Fiction, Fantasy and Horror stories and we can control how the story unfolds and even how it ends.

Look for the next *YOU are the Hero* novel, **The Keys 2: Awakening**, in spring of 2015.

ABOUT THE AUTHOR

Balogun is the author of the bestselling *Afrikan Martial Arts: Discovering the Warrior Within* and screenwriter / producer / director of the films, *A Single Link, Rite of Passage: Initiation* and *Rite of Passage: The Dentist of Westminster.*

He is one of the leading authorities on Steamfunk – a philosophy or style of writing that combines the African and / or African American culture and approach to life with that of the steampunk philosophy and / or steampunk fiction – and writes about it, the craft of writing, Sword & Soul and Steampunk in general, at http://chroniclesofharriet.com/.

He is author of seven novels – the Steamfunk bestseller, *MOSES: The Chronicles of Harriet Tubman (Books 1 & 2)*; the Urban Science Fiction saga, *Redeemer*; the Sword & Soul epic, *Once*

Upon A Time In Afrika, two Fight Fiction, New Pulp novellas – *A Single Link* and *Fist of Afrika*, the two-fisted Dieselfunk tale, *The Scythe* and the "Choose-Your-Own-Destiny"-style Young Adult novel, *The Keys*. Balogun is also contributing co-editor of two anthologies: *Ki: Khanga: The Anthology* and *Steamfunk*.

Finally, Balogun is the Director and Fight Choreographer of the Steamfunk feature film, *Rite of Passage*, which he wrote based on the short story, *Rite of Passage*, by author Milton Davis.

You can reach him on Facebook at www.facebook.com/Afrikan.Martial.Arts; on Twitter @Baba_Balogun and on Tumblr at www.tumblr.com/blog/blackspeculativefiction.

www.ingramcontent.com/pod-product-compliance
Lightning Source LLC
Chambersburg PA
CBHW060913250626
47159CB00008B/2983